Mouse Trap

Caryn Larrinaga

Timber Ghost Press

Mouse Trap

by Caryn Larrinaga

Published by Timber Ghost Press

Printed in the United States of America

Edited by: Beverly Bernard

Cover Art and Design by: Don Noble of Rooster Republic Press

Interior Design: Timber Ghost Press

Print ISBN: 979-8-9855521-6-4

www.TimberGhostPress.com

For Rob.

Chapter One

A thin ray of light snuck between the heavy curtains in Lennox Scott's living room. It slashed a line across the coffee table and crept up his armchair, petering out against the sunken hollow in his left cheek. He didn't register the warmth. Not even the throbbing aches in his bones could pierce the veil of numbness that covered his body.

He blinked slowly at the television's blank screen. Hadn't it been on earlier? A dim memory of a documentary about the evolution of mobile gaming poked through the fog in his mind, but he couldn't be sure when he'd watched it.

It had been several days since he'd last eaten. His stomach didn't growl or grumble. Donut crumbs littered the floor. He thought about picking them up and decided against it. It was easier to simply sit, and besides, that was what his maid was for.

Gina. She would be here soon to clean the house. Sometime in the next few days, at least. If he could last until then, she would open the curtains and turn on the lights.

If he could last.

This wasn't how he had pictured things ending. A lifetime in the same house, his biggest move the upgrade from his childhood bedroom to his parents' former master suite. He remembered working toward an honors degree and a college scholarship, dreams of a career in electrical engineering.

Not this wasted life.

No, he told himself. It wasn't wasted. The sacrifice had been worth it. It had always been worth it. He hadn't known it then, hadn't even known he was making it at all, but the darker things grew, the more clearly he could see the truth. And as the shadows became more than shadows, he finally heard her.

She was calling to him now. Her voice was young and sweet. It reminded him of Dakota. The voice promised she could bring them together, and he ached to see his sister.

The promise proved impossible to resist. Lennox couldn't wait for the maid. He stirred, summoning what little energy he had remaining, and picked up the notebook that rested against his hip. The crackle of the pen across the paper startled him. It seemed so loud after so many days spent in silence. The words he'd been writing for weeks waited there. Only a few more needed to be added. When he was done, he tore the page out, folded it, and slipped it into an envelope. His dry tongue scraped against the flap.

It didn't feel right sitting there. He stood, joints creaking, and dragged himself up the stairs and into his office. With a deep and shuddering groan, he sank into the high-backed chair at his desk. The green light on his computer faded in and out and in again, mirroring his shallow breaths. Getting here had exhausted him, but now things were as they should be.

Lennox placed the envelope beside his keyboard and frowned. The front was blank. It wouldn't get where it needed to go like that. It needed an address. Hands shaking, he leaned forward and plucked a green pen out of the mug on his desk.

He never uncapped it. A final sigh escaped his lungs before he slumped out of his chair and onto the floor.

Chapter Two

D akota Scott stared out her window at the crawling Atlanta traffic with bleary eyes. She contemplated her aching muscles as she blew on her overly frothed cappuccino. No memories surfaced of pulling anything too hard in the previous night's kickball final, but she also didn't remember much that happened after her team hit the bar to celebrate their win. She rubbed her forehead and vowed to take the phrase "beer league" less seriously next season.

The resulting hangover had kept her in bed until nearly noon, and thin tendrils of nausea wrapped around her stomach. It hadn't been a lie when she texted her boss and told her she felt too crummy to come in. Now, she sipped the coffee until the caffeine woke her up enough to fumble in the box of day-old donuts for a raspberry fritter. She took a bite, swallowed, and stopped.

Something was wrong.

Dakota knew exactly what that something was before she dropped the fritter, which remained connected to her lips by a long, blonde hair. Gagging, she pulled the other end out of her mouth.

It didn't match the short, black-and-purple bob she'd been sporting the last few months, and it had clearly been baked into the center of the fritter like an unwanted surprise. She imagined it slipping into the dough as it dipped into the deep fryer, and she gagged again.

Disgusting as it was, the hair didn't surprise her. Yesterday had been a good day. Today would be a bad one. Ever since she'd been a child, she had sensed that there was a sort of balance in the universe. The scales didn't always stick to measuring one person's happiness against that same person's sorrow. She suspected that any bad stretches in her life were balanced by a proportionally good year for someone else. Like a hangover after a great party, the inedible fritter was the counterweight for her team's victory. It didn't occur to her until her phone rang that it might have been an omen of more ill to come.

Her mother's name appeared on the screen.

"Hey, Mom. Everything okay?"

"Dakota?" Her mother's voice cracked on the last syllable.

"Yeah, I'm here. What's wrong?"

"It's Lennox. He's..."

Anything else her mother wanted to say was drowned out by a long wail. There was a series of scratches and muffled words until her father's voice came through clearly.

"It's okay, Gaelle," her father said to her mother. "Just sit back. Breathe. I'll tell her."

He cleared his throat, and the following pause lasted so long that Dakota was on the verge of shouting at him to spit it out.

At last, he told her, "I don't know how to say this, so I'll just say it. Your brother is dead."

The calmness of his voice undermined his words. They lacked the urgency to push their way through Dakota's sluggish brain. When they finally did, they pounded against Dakota's chest over and over as her heart rate doubled. Her mouth went dry, and her tongue fell flat and useless.

"Are you...." She swallowed. It took effort. "Are you sure?"

"Gina called a few minutes ago," he said, referring to Lennox's weekly maid. "She found him when she got there this morning. He was on the floor, and—"

For the first time in twenty years, Dakota heard her father lose his composure. Kerry Scott was famously unemotional, stoic and reserved, no matter the mood of the occasion. He had unconsciously taught Dakota to do the same. She closed her eyes. She wouldn't break down. If his walls were cracking, her mother had to be well over the edge. Dakota needed to be strong for them, now more than ever.

She wrestled her feelings back into their box and asked, "Do they know what happened? Was he sick?"

"They're not sure. They have to...." His voice faltered, and he cleared his throat again. "Your mother and I are going up to Astoria. We'd like you there to help make the arrangements."

"Of course. I'll get the next flight to Portland."

Her mother's sobs continued in the background as they worked out a few more details. Then, the fog the espresso had banished came rolling back into Dakota's mind.

None of it felt real. She was certain that if she picked up her phone and called Lennox, he would answer. His voice would brighten the moment he realized it was really her on the line, and he would want to hear all about her life.

She would have a lot to tell him. It'd been over a year since she had visited. She'd meant to go back for his birthday, then Christmas, but the hospital had been setting up a new medical records system. Any vacation wouldn't be a vacation, not with the nonstop phone calls and emails. Now that the project was finally behind her, just when she'd been looking forward to her next trip....

Guilt and grief warred within her. She should have taken a break. She should have seen him while she had the chance. Tears brimmed in her eyes as she pulled up flight schedules and booked her ticket. The next flight was soon. She didn't have time for a breakdown.

She barely had time for a much-needed shower.

Her legs, usually stout and sturdy, shook beneath her as she made her way to the windowless bathroom. Flicking the light switch did nothing, but the thought of finding a stepladder and replacing the bulb tugged on her exhausted body and threatened to drag her down to the floor. Instead, she turned on her cell phone flashlight and pointed it at the shower, which illuminated the space just enough for her to see what she was doing.

She washed yesterday's sweat off her skin and inhaled the steamy water, allowing it to chase away the last remnants of her hangover. The heat felt good on her sore muscles, and she lingered there longer than she had time for. Her eyes unfocused on the wet tile wall. The stray strands of hair she'd stuck there after shampooing made abstract patterns in the dim light. A lopsided heart. The twin points of a cat's ears. She tipped her head back and let the hot water pull the conditioner out of her hair. Her gaze drifted to the ceiling, where the corners were untouched by her phone's light.

A pair of silver eyes gazed back.

Her heart gave a single, sharp thud. She blinked. When her brown eyes opened again, the silver ones were gone. She slowly reached behind herself and shut off the water, then backed out onto the bathmat, never once looking away from the dark corner above the shower. Even as she stuffed her toiletries into a travel bag, she watched for glowing circles, chest constricting as she finally turned her back on the darkness and fled the bathroom.

In the bright light from the living room window, she tried to shake off the bolt of fear. Droplets of water sprinkled against the wall.

"Jesus, grow up," she murmured.

It was easy enough to say. And she was grown up. Nearly thirty, for God's sake. So why—*why*—did a pair of imaginary eyes in a dark corner rattle her so much that she wanted to hide beneath her bedspread?

Because, she admitted to herself, she had seen those eyes before. And if she allowed herself to think about it, she would have known exactly why seeing them again had smashed through the barrier surrounding her carefully controlled emotions.

The night she'd stopped seeing them was the night her brother stopped being himself.

Chapter Three

C ompared to Georgia's late summer swelter, the air in Oregon was crisp and cool. Dakota drove from Portland to Astoria with the windows down in her rental car and savored the Pacific air. This close to the ocean, the smell of salt hovered just beneath the heavier scents of wet pines and petrichor. She drove on autopilot, following the familiar path to Lennox's house.

Where she would never see him again.

The thought stuck in her mind like a frog in her throat. He had finally left. Deep down, she'd always known he would only go if he was carried out of the house on a stretcher, but it hadn't felt like an urgent reality. She never thought she would actually have to see it. In her more fanciful moments, she envisioned Lennox finally spreading his wings the way she had and making a life for himself somewhere outside their childhood home. Most of the time, she could put the entire situation out of her mind. But when she was in Astoria, she saw the house for what it was. Whether or not he intended it, those walls had become Lennox's prison.

During Dakota's freshman year of college, her father's doctor recommended Kerry relocate to somewhere warmer and drier. Her parents thought the move might be the moment Lennox finally agreed to step foot outside. But he refused to follow them to Tucson, choosing instead to buy his parents' old house so he could stay where he'd always been. Twice a year, the Scott family returned home to Astoria to visit Lennox.

Never once could they convince him to visit them in return.

She parked on the street a few houses down from his and hiked slowly up the steep sidewalk to give her mind time to clear. Trekking up the hill felt good after the long car ride. It had drizzled that morning; she could smell it. But now the sky was only lightly overcast, and she raised her face to the sunlight filtering through the gray clouds.

The house was one of Astoria's many historic "ladies," a narrow but majestic Queen Anne painted a dusty gray. The two-story home had been charming while Dakota was growing up, but its peeling paint and weedy front walk showed how little Lennox had kept up on things since taking it over.

She paused on the porch. It had a peak-a-boo view of the Columbia River, and she justified lingering there by watching a cargo ship make its way upriver to Portland.

Out here, it was easy to picture Lennox on his couch or slumped in the gaming chair in front of his computer. Once she stepped into that house, it would be impossible not to feel his absence.

The door was locked when she finally tried the handle. She let out a slow breath like a silent whistle. The inevitable had been delayed, at least for a few minutes. She pulled out her phone, checked the time, and dialed her mother.

Her father was the one who picked up. "Hey, kiddo. We're running a little behind. Are you there already?"

"Yep. Mom said two o'clock."

"Sorry. We both feel like we're in a fog, so we stopped for coffee. You still drink vanilla lattes, right?"

Dakota sat on the topmost step and propped her elbows up on her knees. "Thanks, that'd be great."

"You're sure you'll be okay for a few minutes without us?"

"Of course. I can hang out on the porch."

"Porch?" There was a pause. "Are you at the house?"

"Yeah, why?"

"We're heading to the mortuary to see Lennox."

See Lennox.

Dakota's stomach thunked through the wood beneath her. Her mother hadn't mentioned that. When Dakota had called to tell her what time her flight got in to PDX, her mother had said, "We'll meet you there at two."

She hadn't specified where "there" was, and Dakota had assumed it would be the house. As if that wasn't painful enough. She didn't want to assume anything else.

"What do you mean, 'see Lennox'?"

In the background, she heard a girl call, "Kerry? Three lattes to go?"

"Our coffees are ready. Look, we'll just meet you there. I'll text you the address."

He hung up, and Dakota sat there, staring at her phone. If she'd known this was coming, she would have had time to dread it. Process it. Give herself a chance to decide how she wanted to feel about it.

There wasn't time for any of that now. All she could do was fold her apprehension up into a tiny square, swallow it down as deep as it would go, and drive to the address her father sent her.

Her destination was in a strange little pocket downtown where three mortuaries and a church were all nearly kitty-corner from each other. She focused on that, wondering which one had popped up first and what benefit there was to the others following suit.

When she stepped into the lily-scented lobby, she greeted her father with a brief but tight hug. Her mother smiled, but her red eyes and mascara-lined cheeks betrayed what she'd been doing all the way from the airport.

"My baby." Her mother pulled Dakota into her arms and clung to her for a while.

To the mortuary staff, they might have looked like a mismatched pair. Even with the natural shrinking of age, Gaelle Scott towered over her daughter. Her already thin frame had tipped into frailty some years before, while Dakota's thickened from season after season of casual sports. Gaelle hadn't been able to pass her Haitian genes on to her adopted children, but her fierce love swirled around Dakota as much as any other mother's.

"Where are you staying?" Gaelle asked.

"At the Elliott."

"Why don't you stay at the Hampton with us, save some money? We can get a rollaway."

Dakota smiled. She made a good living as a software analyst, but her parents still worried about her financial situation. She suspected they would never stop. And hotel costs or not, there was the unspoken expectation that none of them would choose to stay in Lennox's house rather than incur that expense.

"I can afford it, Mom. Besides, I like it there. It's right by tons of good restaurants."

A middle-aged man in a well-cut black suit cleared his throat and dragged the women out of their comfortable chitchat about lodging and food. With that single stuttering sound, he hitched them firmly to the awful reason they'd come here.

Introductions were made, and the Scotts followed the mortuary assistant down a flight of stairs to a white-tiled basement. Dakota's feet grew heavier with every step. The smell in the air shifted from funerary flowers to sharp disinfectant, with the faintest lingering tendrils of flame and ash. Each inhale further emphasized the undeniable reminder of what they were about to see. By the time they stepped into the preparation room and saw the sheet-covered table, she was on the verge of fainting.

"Are you ready?" the assistant asked.

Abso-freaking-lutely not, Dakota wanted to shout. But the solemn nods from both her parents were all it took for the assistant to pull back the sheet.

Dakota only saw Lennox for an instant before reflexively whipping her head to the side, but that was enough. His image was scarred into her mind. It glowed against the darkness when she closed her eyes. Slowly, one breath at a time, she forced herself to look again.

God, when had he gotten so skinny? The man in front of her was bizarrely aged, as though a much older Lennox had travelled back through time and taken her brother's place. Gaunt cheeks. Thin hair. The very definition of skin and bones. Lennox had only been thirty-four, but there on that table, with just his head and the sharp edges of his shoulders visible, he looked older than their father. A sudden certainty broke through the swirling mass of grief and panic that was overtaking her mind.

Lennox had wasted away into nothing. And once he was cremated, he would literally turn to dust.

Her mother fell to her knees, knuckles white against the metal preparation table. Her father gripped his wife's shoulders. His jaw worked up and down, as though he wanted to say something. Dakota wondered if he wanted to scream. Her eyes pooled with tears, and she bit down on her curled finger to stop herself from sobbing and making her mother feel even worse.

You should have been there. A whisper, so soft and mellow that she was sure it came from within her own mind, floated through the room. *You should have seen this coming, made him see a doctor about whatever made this happen. You could have saved him.*

This is your fault.

Without a word, Dakota spun around and fled up the stairs.

Chapter Four

The inside of Lennox's house had changed little in the last year. The living room was spotlessly clean and sparsely furnished with the things her parents hadn't wanted to take to Arizona. Through the arched doorway to the kitchen, neatly arranged appliances stood atop speckled granite counters, and she knew without checking that the fridge would be filled with the ingredients for complex, international dishes. Even so, something was off.

She couldn't decide what it was until her father moved to the front window and threw open the heavy embroidered curtains covering it. Light flooded inside, reflecting off the mirror above the fireplace to further brighten the room. It had been dark, Dakota realized. It was never dark in Lennox's house. It felt wrong. She moved through the room, turning on the lamps.

When she looked around again, the room looked so much like the way it had years ago, before everything changed, that her heart ached. She could suddenly hear laughter bouncing off the walls and see three children sitting around the coffee table playing a board game. There she was, seven years old and already cheating, slipping ones from beneath the Monopoly board and into her disorganized stack of money. Lennox had been eleven then. Either he didn't see her petty larceny or he pretended not to, focusing instead on helping their baby brother Kai—sweet, innocent Kai—roll the dice.

All at once, she felt like a child again. It wasn't a good feeling. Her unease rose, and a sudden fear of the dark wiggled up her scalp. Lennox had added a few spotlights since taking over the house, and four high-wattage bulbs blasted the shadows out of the corners when she turned them on.

Light. The whole house needed it. In the kitchen, she yanked curtains back and flicked every switch, even the one above the stove. She stalked down the short hallway, ignoring the never-opened door to the basement, and threw open the door to what had been her parents' bedroom. There, her nostalgia vanished.

This room didn't look, feel, or smell anything like it had when they were younger. She'd never once stepped foot into it since Lennox took it over. Like the living room, dark curtains covered both windows. She wanted to walk into the room and open them. She wanted to slide her hand up the wall and turn on the overhead light.

Not yet. The light will chase away more than darkness. Give this place more time to hold his memory.

That was easier to do than cross the threshold. She stepped back and closed the door.

When she climbed the stairs, gentle sobs drifted out of the bedroom to her right. Dakota's fingers curled slowly around the doorframe, and as she leaned around it, her chest constricted.

Her parents perched on the edge of Kai's little toddler bed. Her father's arm cradled her mother's shoulders as she cried. Around them, Kai's room was much the same as it had been when he died. Stenciled dinosaurs covered both sides of the steeply peaked ceiling. Berenstain Bears books filled the tiny shelf beneath the window. Kai's most treasured possessions had traveled to Arizona with his parents, but the rest remained here, standing as monuments to the time before his death had broken the Scott family into pieces.

Dakota left them, hoping to escape their grief by peeking in on her old room. It was much emptier than Kai's but nearly as much a shrine to her teenaged self, with everything she hadn't needed in college still in place. The queen bed Lennox kept for Dakota's visits looked enticingly soft.

Couldn't you use a nap? Lay down. Stay for a while.

But no. Dakota was a woman on a mission. A driving need to light all their childhood bedrooms propelled her forward to the largest one, and she paused once more in the doorway to one of Lennox's private spaces.

He had converted his old room into an office. A green light glowed in the darkness from atop the tall computer tower. Not much had changed here, either. Mario posters decorated the walls, and collectible figurines were carefully arranged on mounted shelves. Apart from the bed and dresser he'd moved downstairs, the rest of the furniture was the same as he'd used as a child, down to the Legend of Zelda overworld map on the floor.

Unlike the master bedroom, she'd been in here many times before as an adult, legs folded beneath herself in the recliner in the corner. She had enjoyed sitting there while she was in town, reading a book while Lennox worked, listening to his fingertips clacking away on the mechanical keyboard and his deep voice muttering about code deployments. Being near him was warm. Now his absence made her shiver.

Her father's hand rested on her shoulder. "Cold, kiddo?"

"A little, yeah."

"I think we're all used to hotter weather. Come on. I'll light the stove."

Dakota turned and stared up at her father. He hadn't shaved. Gray, seldom-seen stubble covered his jaw and chin in irregular patches, and his dark eyes were strained and tired.

"What are you going to do with the house?" she asked. "All of Lennox's stuff?"

A smile softened his face. "That's for you to decide. He left all of it to you."

Chapter Five

T he three of them huddled around Lennox's kitchen table. Dakota's father slid a folded sheet of paper toward her.

"This is a copy of Lennox's will," he said. "The original is being probated."

Dakota unfolded the paper and skimmed it. It was a short, simple document, and her father had used an orange highlighter on the key passage.

Disposition of Property

The entirety of my personal property, including my home and all possessions therein, shall be distributed to my sister, Dakota Scott. Everything to which I belong to shall be hers.

She lifted her gaze from the will. "Is this real?"

"Completely. I checked with the notary who witnessed Lennox's signature. It's valid."

"Does it say anything about his funeral? What he wants us to do?"

"No, just that we should pay for it out of his savings before the money is distributed to you."

The will fluttered in her shaking hands. Her father's words were bouncing off her brain, not yet sinking in. "Where did you get this?"

Her mother's shoulders began quaking anew. Her father gripped her hand atop the table.

"He emailed it to me last week." He paused. "From the timing, we think he might have known this was coming."

"I wish he'd told us," her mother said in a small voice. "If he knew, why wouldn't he tell me?"

Dakota had the same question. Did Lennox know? How? Had he been sick? No, if he knew he was sick, he would have told their parents. He would have told her.

Why would he? You hardly ever called. It's been over a year since you stepped foot in this house. Did you really think he wouldn't notice when you stopped caring?

"I did care," she whispered, too quietly for her parents to hear over the sound of her mother sobbing.

She had lied to herself about many things over the years, but that was the truth. She loved Lennox. It had been a transition, getting used to the shy and withdrawn person he'd become in high school, but he'd never stopped being her brother. He'd never stopped looking out for her.

If he had just been willing to come to her, if he'd been willing to leave his house at all, they would have seen each other more. And it wasn't like he was calling her every week.

Dakota straightened her back as she successfully crumpled her guilt into a tiny black ball and let it sink down to her toes. If they'd grown apart in the last year, it was on Lennox. Not her.

"What will you do with the house?" her father asked.

Through the thick layer of pain that coated his expression, Dakota saw the barest hint of relief. She envied him. Everything lay squarely on her shoulders. The burden of dealing with Lennox's things, of emptying the house and selling it off—

She blinked. That was one decision made.

"I'm going to sell it," she said. "And everything in it."

Her father nodded. "I think that's for the best."

Abruptly, her mother leapt to her feet. Tears flowed freely down her face. "I can't do this." Without another word, she pushed her way through the back door and nearly tumbled down the steps.

With a sigh, her father watched the door slam closed. "She's upset that we're not more upset."

Dakota frowned. "I *am* upset."

"I know, kiddo. But you and I have always been the calm ones about this kind of thing. She's never understood that just because someone isn't wearing their heart on their sleeve, that doesn't mean it isn't broken."

A thick lump clogged Dakota's throat. She held up a hand to her father to stop him from rising. "I'll go. I haven't really talked to her about... you know. Any of it."

She found her mother standing at the back corner of the house. Behind her, the detached garage slumped, sad and empty. In front of her, a steep stairwell led to the basement door. Her mother's eyes were locked on the damp square of concrete at the foot of the steps, where that morning's rainwater drained through a small metal grate.

Lennox had told her once that the stairwell hadn't always been surrounded by the wrought-iron railing. Their parents had installed it and the low access gate when they adopted her as a toddler. Her fascination with the stairs was never-ending, and their mother was terrified she would hurt herself trying to climb down them. Dakota ran her fingers over the gate's latch, now rusted and flimsy with no padlock to hold it in place.

"It was my fault," her mother said suddenly.

Dakota didn't need to ask what she meant. Softly, she told her, "It wasn't, Mom. It was nobody's fault."

"No. I was there, ten feet inside. I shouldn't have left him, not even for—" Gaelle turned to face Dakota. Her lower lip trembled. "It was just the cookies. The timer went off, and Kai loved them when they were soft and gooey. I thought he would be fine. If the gate had been locked...."

She trailed off. Dakota already knew what she was going to say. That she'd been sure the gate was locked; she always double-checked it. That just as she was pulling the baking sheet out of the oven, she heard the squeak of metal hinges and dropped the cookies onto the floor.

By the time she got outside, it was too late.

Dakota stared down the steps. She'd been eight when it happened, but that was old enough for every image of Kai at the top of the back steps to carve itself into her memory. As fascinated as Lennox claimed Dakota had been with the stairs, Kai was downright obsessed. He had a love-hate relationship with the basement entrance. Anytime they were in the backyard, he stood at the gate, tiny hands wrapped around the twisting metal balusters as he stared at something only he could see. He tried several times to fit his little blond head through the gaps, always discouraged by a sharp word from their parents.

She had asked him about it one day, pressing her small face against the cold bars beside his and peering into the darkness. It irritated her that she couldn't see anything. "What's down there?"

"Listen," Kai lisped.

Dakota tried. She strained her ears, but all she could hear was the laughter of their parents behind them as they grilled hotdogs for dinner and the steady *thud, thud* from Lennox's basketball on the driveway. She grew frustrated in less than a minute and gave up.

"This is boring," she complained.

Kai held a finger up to his lips. "Shhh. She can hear you."

"Who?"

"The Whisper Lady." He wrapped his chubby fist around the bar again and fixed his wide-eyed gaze back on the shadows at the bottom of the stairs. "She wants me to find her."

"Can I help?"

"No. She doesn't like you." Kai shivered. "I don't like her."

"Kids!" their mother called. "Go wash your hands. It's time for dinner."

Dakota was bored with Kai's game anyway, and she pushed back from the gate and went inside. Like her parents, she didn't think he would ever manage to get down the stairs and find whatever he was looking for. The railing kept him safe. The gate kept him from harm.

Until it didn't.

By the time their neighbor had collected Lennox and Dakota from school on that awful day, Kai no longer lay at the bottom of the steps. Only his discarded G.I. Joe doll remained, abandoned in the turtle-shaped sandbox in which he'd been playing when Gaelle went inside.

Now grief stirred in Dakota's chest. She imagined her little brother's body crumpled outside the basement door, cold and broken. She tried to wipe the mental slate clean and brush the image away along with her emotions, but they clung there as stubbornly as darkness clung to the wet concrete walls.

Something moved in those shadows. A sound like the shifting of dried leaves whispered up the steps. It was so quiet that Dakota wasn't even sure she'd heard it, but she squinted and leaned forward.

Two bright slits squinted back.

Dakota's mind short-circuited. She lost her balance, stumbling forward and catching herself on the railing.

"What are you doing?" Her mother grabbed her by the back of her shirt and tugged her away from the stairs.

Dakota looked from her mother's angry eyes to the drain. The slits were gone. Only darkness remained. "Did you see that?"

"See what?"

"The...."

As she tried to conjure the words to describe the things that may or may not have actually been there, she fully registered the expression on her mother's face. The top layer of anger was only a fine sheen. Beneath it, fear and pain churned. Dakota hadn't seen her mother this way—so raw, completely submerged in sorrow—since she was a child.

"Nothing," Dakota finished weakly.

"Don't scare me like that." Her mother shuddered. "Let's go inside. I can't stand it out here."

As she turned to follow her mother around the corner of the house, Dakota glanced back at the basement entrance. Nothing moved. Nothing shone in the darkness. But she couldn't shake the feeling that something had been down there.

Kai.

No, it couldn't be. Ghosts didn't exist. Lennox had proved that to her twenty years before. If her baby brother was anywhere, it would be a brighter place than this. He wouldn't linger here.

And soon, she hoped, neither would she.

Chapter Six

What remained of the Scott family planned Lennox's services from the same mortuary where he'd been cremated. It was easier coming here for a second time, knowing that she wouldn't have to go back down to the lower level and see her brother's emaciated body. It brought her a sense of comfort and finality to know that his remains now rested in a temporary urn instead of on a cold metal table.

The staff set the family up in a small room furnished with deep leather couches and marble-topped tables. It felt somber yet luxurious, and the staff guided them through checklists and catalogs with discreet prices. Some of it went quickly. There was already room in the family plot. Kerry and Gaelle immediately selected a deep blue ceramic urn that reminded them of Lennox's eyes. Using one of the mortuary's templates, they managed to write his obituary in under an hour. But the three of them floundered when it came to the service itself. Memorials, funerals, celebrations of life, wakes—the options were overwhelming.

They ran out of emotional stamina on their first visit and had to come back for a second.

Dakota was sure these decisions were never easy, but they felt even more difficult in light of the life Lennox had led. His maid, Gina, joined them at the mortuary to help them finalize their decisions. They might be his closest family, but she was the only person who saw Lennox regularly enough to have a deep understanding of his life.

In a fit of gallows humor, Dakota said, "If Lennox were planning his own funeral, he would host it right in his living room."

"I don't think so." Gina tapped a pen on the end of her nose as she gave the idea serious consideration. "A few friends came over sometimes, but almost everything in his life was virtual. He lived in that office. If he wasn't working, he was playing Ultra Quest Online." She tucked her red curls behind her ears. "If he was in charge of this deal, he'd have it in some made-up tavern in that game."

"Out of the question," Gaelle said. "I'm not mourning my son in a computer."

"If I may..." The funeral director smiled kindly and folded his hands over his crossed knees. "As much as we want the services to honor Lennox's memory, I always like to remind our clients that funerals are for the living. As Lennox left no last wishes about his memorial, consider the things you loved about him and think about how we might celebrate those aspects of his life and personality."

After a long pause, Gaelle offered, "He cared about everyone around him, ever since he was a little boy. He was so thrilled when we grew our family. All he wanted was more siblings to take care of."

Dakota's throat tightened.

"He did that with his online friends, too," Gina put in. "He told me he liked being the healer so he could make sure everybody survived."

The funeral director made a note in his binder. "He sounds like he was a truly wonderful man."

Remorse tugged Dakota deeper into the couch.

Your brother cared deeply about his family, and how did you all repay him? By scattering across the country and leaving him alone fifty weeks out of the year.

"So, what are we thinking?" their funerary concierge asked. "Graveside service?"

Gaelle and Kerry looked helplessly at their daughter. Dakota sighed. It seemed that this, as with everything else, was up to her to decide.

Lennox had left her everything because he cared about her. Like their parents, he worried needlessly about her finances. He wanted her to be okay. And suddenly, she knew exactly how they could honor his generous spirit.

She straightened up. "We'll have a wake. At Blaylock's. Food, cocktails, everything'll be on Lennox. He'd want to make sure his friends all have a great time, right?"

They pushed forward with the idea, leaning on Gina to help them pull the guest list together. Dakota marveled at her. They'd been in the same graduating class, but all she remembered about Gina was the gossip when she dropped out of college freshman year to have a baby—*gasp*—out of wedlock. Dakota hadn't even known Gina was Lennox's maid until she called the Scotts to let them know he had died. Now here she was, coming to Dakota's rescue at every turn.

Gina's knowledge of Lennox's life ate at Dakota as she walked to her hotel. Would Dakota have known that much if she'd stayed in Astoria? Would she have been better equipped for all of this if she hadn't chosen money over family and bolted to a big city for the best paying job she could find?

The answers waited for her in her hotel room, calling out from the dark corners before she turned on the lights.

He deserved a better sister than you were ever willing to be.

Chapter Seven

The graveside service immediately overwhelmed Dakota's emotions. She'd thought she had come to terms with it, that she had accepted her brother's death once she saw his body, but the sight of the newly dug grave threw her mind beneath a thick blanket of denial like a child hiding from a monster in the closet. That wasn't Lennox in the polished urn. They weren't about to lower him into the ground, where he would only be visited on Memorial Day and his birthday.

If even then. He was the only reason you ever came back here. Now he'll be like Kai, abandoned and forgotten.

The voice rose from the dark place that awaited Lennox's remains, but the criticism had been on the edge of Dakota's mind since stepping foot in the cemetery. Lennox's headstone wouldn't be ready for several weeks, but beside his grave, a narrow tombstone marked the place where Kai had been laid to rest. The flowers Dakota had left on her last visit were long gone. How often would she come here now that Lennox was gone, too?

You could stay. It would be easy. You already have the house.

It was true. And she loved it here. Vibrant as Atlanta was, it had nothing on her hometown. The air was clean, clear, and alive with the energy of the flowing waters around her. Even in the cemetery, she could glimpse the wide, slow waters of Youngs River through the towering pines. Sure, she would leave years of friendships behind in Georgia, but she could pick up some pieces here. Start with Gina, find an adult sports league, build her own community.

She could probably even keep her job. It wasn't like she treated patients. She could configure software from anywhere. Go remote, work from the same upstairs office where Lennox had spent his life—

A shudder ran down her body.

No. None of it would work. She couldn't bear spending all her time in Lennox's house. Even the few minutes here and there with her parents had been difficult. The walls were soaked with the heavy energy from his sad, solitary life. She would sell the house and use the money to buy a condo in Atlanta, and that was final.

Before she knew it, the service had concluded. She'd spent the entirety of it in the comfort of assessment and logistics, safely cocooned away from the distress of the moment.

The gathered mourners each laid a rose beside Lennox's grave. Dakota followed her mother's example and bent down to rest two kissed fingertips on the urn. That minor act nearly shattered the wall around Dakota's emotions, and she barely managed to rein them in before straightening.

As they walked down the slope to their cars, Gina fell into step beside Dakota and looped their arms together.

"Want a ride to the bar?" Gina asked.

Dakota glanced at the black town car waiting for her mother and father. If she climbed into it with them, the force of her parents' grief would be too close. She would break down, and that would push her mother further over the edge. "That'd be great, thanks."

They rode in silence in Gina's SUV for a full five minutes. From the corner of her eye, Dakota noticed Gina's hands gently twisting the steering wheel and cringed. She could feel something coming. There was something Gina was dying to say.

"I'm sorry," Gina finally blurted. "I was trying to give you a respectful silence or whatever, but the quiet drives me bananas. Do you mind if I turn on the radio?"

Dakota cracked a relieved smile. "Trust me, the last thing I want is to wallow in peace over here."

She tried to remember if Gina was a talker, and realized that she hadn't paid her much attention in high school. Gina wasn't into sports and Dakota wasn't into... well, whatever it was besides sports that Gina or anyone else took an interest in. Gina parked, and as they walked to the bar, Dakota studied her. She had a long, willowy figure, with thin but muscular arms. A dancer, Dakota decided.

"What have you been up to since high school?" Dakota asked.

"Not much. You probably know I got pregnant right when college started." Gina shot Dakota a grin. "Allie was a rush-week baby."

"Did you marry her dad?"

"Nah. I didn't really know him. And I had enough going on with being pregnant. I didn't want to have to worry about getting married, too. My parents were happy about that part. They didn't want to deal with some son-in-law who was only there out of obligation. And they've been over the moon for Allie since she got here."

They reached the bar, and raucous laughter exploded out of the heavy door as soon as Dakota pulled it open. The intimate space was already packed. Many of Lennox's online friends had flown in, both to pay their respects to their fallen guild-mate and to meet one another face-to-face for the first time. It felt as much like a reunion as a wake, and Dakota knew it would have thrilled her brother to host all his friends in his hometown like this. It certainly wasn't her parents' scene, but they'd had the graveside service.

This part was all for Lennox.

His photo sat in a place of honor at the bar. It was a few years old, taken when he still had broad shoulders and carried weight in his smiling cheeks. His light hair was combed severely back into a ponytail that draped over one shoulder, and the top of his gaming chair was just visible behind him. Dakota guessed it had been taken with a webcam, probably for work.

Dakota's father had displayed more presence of mind than she'd done when packing for this trip by tucking a few wall frames into his suitcase. Pre-teen Lennox showed off his braces in a wide grin as he hugged Dakota in front of Astor Elementary on her first day of kindergarten. A candid shot captured all three Scott children hunting for Easter eggs in the park, and a slightly crooked photo of the whole family at Cape Disappointment reminded Dakota of her father's defective tripod with the slowly collapsing left leg. Her nostalgic smile faded as she realized these were all taken before Lennox turned fifteen—before their parents started having to drag him out of the house if they needed to take him anywhere.

It took her a while to figure out why the row of pictures ended with an illustration of a green-skinned man wearing heavy armor and holding an axe. Just as she realized it must have been Lennox's character in his favorite online game, a short man with deep smile lines lifted a glass of whiskey toward it.

Voice booming, he addressed the packed bar. "To Lentropy the Paladin, who was always first through the door and never left anyone behind."

"To Lentropy!" the others chorused, raising their glasses.

"This is amazing," Dakota told Gina. "I can't believe you pulled this all together so fast."

Gina nodded toward the man who'd made the toast. "That was all Quinn. He used to work with Lennox and got him into Ultra Quest."

Dakota stood beside the bar with her parents in an impromptu receiving line, meeting Lennox's friends and accepting their condolences. All of them were from the internet. He'd dropped out of Astoria High junior year and quickly lost contact with everyone from school. Learning to code and doing freelance work swallowed up all his time and energy. Eventually, his skills earned him a place at a software company. Between that and online games, he hardly had to leave his computer.

Her happiness that he'd found so many people to play with warred with her guilt that she wasn't one of them. But after staring at a computer all day at work, she spent as much time away from electronics and out in the fresh air as she could.

Why didn't you at least try? Even for an hour a week? You're so selfish.

When they were younger, Lennox loved playing board games. Monopoly, Clue, Mouse Trap, and Trouble were household favorites, and when she was a little older, he cajoled her into playing Risk. One four-hour game was all he got out of her before she swore off the tiny military figures for good.

She frowned, trying to remember if she'd seen any of those old games in his house. They had to be somewhere. He'd kept her room in nearly the same state she'd left it. She couldn't picture him throwing away anything related to their childhood memories. And if he had tossed them out, it would have been a great excuse to take him to one of the new gaming shops in town.

He wouldn't have gone. Their mother had hauled him to doctor and dental appointments as a teenager, but did he take care of his own health that way as an adult? Did he go to bars or restaurants? See a barber? From the way he'd looked at the mortuary, she didn't picture him eating out much or engaging in any level of self-care.

Dakota's stamina ran out long before Lennox's friends'. Her parents were equally exhausted, and they found her sagging on a barstool with a Dr Pepper.

"Are you sober?" her mother asked.

"Yeah." She didn't explain that if she drank, she would cry, and she was saving that for the privacy of her hotel room. The last thing she wanted was this gaggle of strangers seeing her get emotional.

"We're heading out. Part of me feels like we should be the last to leave, but..." Her mother gazed around at the gamers, who were growing louder with every round, and shrugged. "I think they'll carry on valiantly without us."

Dakota slid off the stool and stood on tired legs. "Oh, thank God. I'll sneak out with you."

"Before you go, could you do us a favor?"

"Sure, what do you need?"

Her mother carefully picked up the framed photo of Lennox at his computer and held it out to Dakota. "I want to take this home, but I'm worried the glass will break in my luggage. Could you take it back to the house with the other mementos? We can ship it with the rest of what we're keeping."

Dakota wanted to ask, *Why can't you do it?* But she didn't trust herself to keep any trace of petulance out of her voice. Her parents had gone through enough today. She could do them this small favor. As they slipped out of the bar, she went to the entrance and began collecting the cards and photos Lennox's friends had left for the family.

Gina was chatting with Quinn nearby and caught sight of what Dakota was doing. She raised her voice above the din, calling, "Last call for the guest book, everybody! If you haven't signed it, do it now."

The bar thoughtfully provided a tote bag, and Gina helped pack everything into it.

"Thank you," Dakota said with feeling. "We couldn't have done any of this without you."

"It's no problem. I meant to ask you earlier—you're selling Lennox's house, right?"

"Yeah, you want to buy it?"

Gina laughed. "I couldn't afford that neighborhood. But if you want, I offer a deep-cleaning service to get places ready to go on the market. I'll give you a friends and family discount."

"You don't have to do that. The discount, I mean. But yeah, that'd be amazing."

They made plans for Gina to come the next day, and Dakota finally wobbled out of the bar with the mementos in tow. She walked around the block to her hotel and slid behind the wheel of her rental car. Her body was drained and her mind teetered on the edge of numbness, but she couldn't rest. Not yet.

And neither could anything else.

Chapter Eight

The curtains were drawn again when Dakota got back to the house. No light shone through them, and the porch light was off. She made a mental note to ask her parents to leave the lights on if they were the last ones out the door and let herself into the cold, lifeless space.

Someone waited for her in the shadows.

Dakota leapt backward and slammed her hand across the light switch. Her own reflection, wide-eyed and terrified, stared back at her from the mirror above the fireplace.

Got you, it seemed to say.

She had no idea where to put the tote bag of mementos. Her gaze was foggy as she stared through the doorway to the dark kitchen and down the hallway to Lennox's room. Neither of those options made sense, and she didn't have the energy to climb the stairs unless she was sure there was a good reason.

What else would her parents want shipped to them? They'd already taken what they wanted from Kai's room.

Would they want things from Lennox's living room? His office?

Certainly not the basement.

After a few moments of turning slowly in the living room, she gave up and sat on the couch. The cards and photos slid onto the coffee table as she dumped out the tote bag. She smiled sadly as she thumbed through the glossy drugstore prints. None of them had been taken in person. All of them were screenshots.

She closed her eyes and leaned back against the cushions. Above her, one of the spotlights flashed and flicked before the bulb went out and its corner went dark. Something there stirred, unseen.

Of course no one has any photos. What, do you think Gina snapped some pics when she came to clean? And how about you? You carry a camera around in your pocket wherever you go, but you didn't take pictures here, not even selfies, and never with Lennox.

It was true. She never had the urge to take photos when she visited. Every trip was the same. What would she capture apart from the colorful meals Lennox made with all of his kitchen gadgets? They weren't making new memories or having fresh adventures.

But whose fault is that? Certainly not his. You knew his limitations. You could have brought excitement with you when you came, but you just sunk down to his energy level and lolled around the house. Pathetic.

She had never understood why Lennox tethered himself to the house by an invisible umbilical cord. He hadn't always been that way. As kids, they would ride their bikes to the park and play on the swings. Their parents took them to the theater for every single Disney movie. He'd never fought any of that.

Until he was fourteen.

Their entire family had changed that year. Kai's death traumatized all of them, and for months, she was sure none of them would ever know happiness again. Every shadow scared her, and she developed a debilitating fear of the dark.

It was Lennox who had helped her with that. He always protected her, even from the darkness inside herself. He boosted her up the metaphorical wall between the shock of losing Kai and the chance to enjoy her own childhood. Her parents began to climb out of the black hole of their grief at the same time, never fully emerging, but no longer swallowed up by sorrow.

For whatever reason, Lennox sunk deeper into the quicksand and never fought to get out. Dakota moved forward. Lennox stayed behind.

He stayed in this house for twenty years. The least you can do is stay a few days. Be present. Commit yourself to dealing with Lennox's things and resolving what he left unsettled. You owe him.

Her eyelids fluttered open. She stared at the ceiling. That idea—*you owe him*—tried to flit in and out of her mind like any passing thought, but she seized it and held on. She did owe Lennox. She had never thought about why. If she did, the guilt of carrying on with her own life while Lennox was stuck here would bubble up and overflow like Mentos in a Diet Coke. She had sensed the debt, but Lennox never said anything. He simply stayed.

You can stay, too.

She could. And she would. All she needed to do was go down to the Elliott, get her things, check out, come back....

But before she could get up again, her exhaustion tipped her onto her side, and she fell asleep.

Welcome home, Dakota.

Chapter Nine

D akota opened her eyes in her old bedroom. She lay on top of the faded pink quilt, limbs aching and head pounding. Despite not drinking, she felt hung over. It was from the grief, she decided. There had to be a name for that. She could invent one if her damn head would stop acting like somebody had smashed it with a frying pan.

She rolled over and tried to check the time. Her phone screen stubbornly stayed black, and she sighed. Her charger was back at the hotel, but Lennox had to have one around here somewhere.

As she stood, her body felt weak and sluggish. It got easier as she went, and she stretched her arms above her head on the landing. Lennox's office was right beside her room. It was the most logical place for a charger to be, but her feet carried her down the stairs and into the living room.

A board game waited on the coffee table. She drew closer and sank to the carpet on her knees.

Mouse Trap. One of her favorites. There had been solid weeks when her mother didn't bother telling them to put the box away. It would be pointless. Five minutes later, the game would come right down off the shelf for them to play again.

She raised the lid and rested it, artwork side up, on the table. Out came the board and all the colorful plastic pieces. She toyed with her favorite piece, the little blue basket that would jerk down the pole and trap the mouse inside.

Slowly, she started putting the mechanism together.

"That's cheating," Lennox said, his voice still making its way down to the deep bass it would eventually become.

Dakota raised her head. Her brother sat across from her, his light hair thick and messy. His tone was as stern as any fourteen-year-old boy could muster, but his eyes were kind and his grin was teasing.

She tossed a pigtail over her shoulder and went back to fitting the pieces together. Her hands were too small and her fingers too stubby for her to manage some of them, but she stubbornly pulled them away from Lennox when he tried to help. "I can do it."

He rested an elbow on the low table and propped his chin on his palm. "You know that's not how you're supposed to play it. We have to go around the board and build it together. Then I'll trap your mouse, and I'll win."

"No, I'll win. You watch. Give me your mouse."

A shadow moved across the room.

Lennox's face clouded over. "We shouldn't be playing with this. It was a mistake."

"But I want to play."

"No." He yanked the board away and dismantled what little she'd accomplished.

Dakota's eyes filled with tears. "You're mean."

"I'm not mean. I'm nice, the nicest person you'll ever know. You'll see. Give me that."

He ripped the blue cage out of her hand. Once all the pieces were back in the box, he lifted the lid off the table and moved to put it in place. With her short torso barely taller than the table, Dakota glimpsed something written inside the lid.

"What is that?" she asked.

"Nothing."

"Let me see." She tugged on the lid, trying to flip it over. There'd been something on it. She had opened the game dozens of times, and the inside of the lid had only ever been plain gray cardboard. It was different now.

"Stop it, Dakota!"

Lennox held his ground. Dakota set her jaw and pulled stubbornly. Their standstill was broken when the edge of the box tore where Dakota's pudgy fingers gripped it, and she went flying backward into the couch.

She woke with a start beneath the covers in her bedroom. The room was pitch black, but she could feel the little yarn ties on the quilt. Groaning, she rolled out of bed and turned on the lamp. Her body ached beneath yesterday's clothing as she shuffled across the carpet and opened the curtains. She could use a shower. As she pictured herself letting warm water run down her body, the thought of liquid made her throat scratch and complain.

Her feet were halfway down the stairs before she remembered her dream. She took the last few steps slowly, allowing the living room to come into view a foot at a time until she could see the coffee table.

It was empty.

Dakota frowned. For a moment, she'd felt certain Mouse Trap would be there. She had been prepared to explain its presence away as part of some kind of stress-induced sleepwalking, and now that it wasn't waiting for her, she felt strangely disappointed. She wanted to find it.

Dry throat forgotten, she turned around and searched upstairs. Her fingers walked down rows of video game boxes on the shelves in Lennox's office, but it wasn't there. The quest took her back downstairs. She found a few board games in the TV stand's narrow cupboards, but she didn't recognize any of the titles from her childhood.

She drummed her fingers on a colorful-looking game called Castle Ravenloft and thought. If this were her house—which, she supposed, it was—she didn't think she would keep a bunch of old games in her bedroom. But she wouldn't have made a lot of the choices Lennox had. She went down the hallway and paused in front of his door. Just like it had her first day here, it felt like trespassing to step inside. But her need to find the game overrode her childhood programming to stay out of the master bedroom. With a deep breath, she went in.

It was cleaner than she expected. His room was the worst of everyone's when they were kids. Clothes, half-completed Lego sets, handheld video games, and books had littered the floor back then. But Lennox had shed his pigsty tendencies as he got older. His bedroom had less clutter and furniture than even her hotel room. Only a bed, a dresser, a nightstand, and three floor lamps stood around the edges of the space. A night-light shaped like a pair of dice was plugged into the wall. In the closet, video game and band t-shirts were organized by color on a row of hangers. The room had zero personality, no sense at all that it had belonged to her brother. All of that was reserved for his office upstairs, and she suspected he slept in the recliner up there more often than he slept in his bed.

Grief dragged her downward like a weighted blanket. She had expected to spend a week here sifting through Lennox's things and agonizing over what to keep and what to donate. But he had lived as simply as a monk. Everything from his social life to his most prized possessions had lived in the virtual world. He'd kept little of it in the house.

Maybe not. There's one place you haven't checked. Where better to store the most important things than the basement?

A chill slithered up Dakota's spine. The basement. She hadn't been down there in.... Well, she couldn't actually remember. Not since Kai died. Not since the grief plowed over her parents' dreams and salted the earth until no desire to grow their family remained.

Don't be scared. It's just a basement. And the game is down there. You know it is.

Slowly, she forced her feet to take her to the basement door. It stood there, just a slab of unvarnished pine with a tarnished brass knob. But as her fingertips touched the cool metal, a fear she hadn't felt since she was eight years old rushed up through her arm and into her throat. Dakota covered her mouth, dashed into the kitchen, and vomited clear bile into the sink.

Body trembling, she stood with her back against the counter and stared at the basement door. Whatever Lennox had put down there, she didn't have the strength to see it.

Chapter Ten

It took Dakota's limbs a while to stop shaking. Eventually, she regained the ability to walk around without looking like a lost drunkard. She decided the best way to celebrate this recovery was with breakfast. But unlike Lennox, she was no chef. If she wanted good food, she would have to go find it.

She paused in front of the row of little hooks next to the door. Her rental car key hung there beside Lennox's house key. His was hardly used, sharp and shiny on the miniature computer mouse key chain she'd gotten him for his birthday. For a moment, she considered combining the two rings to make it easier to carry both keys at a time. But her fingers just wouldn't do it. Her brain refused to send the signals to them to make them try. Even though the car key wasn't really hers, it still felt too permanent to add Lennox's to it, like she was taking possession of the house in a real and lasting way.

Unwilling to pick up both keys at once, she decided to just walk. There was a coffee shop a few blocks away, and a slow stroll in the fresh air would clear her head as much as the caffeine would.

Just as she grabbed Lennox's key, the front door swung open into her feet.

"Oh!" Her father's eyebrows were high on his forehead. "Sorry, kiddo. Didn't see you there. Coffee?"

She took the latte gratefully and stepped out of the way. Besides hot coffee and fresh pastries, her parents had brought a small stack of boxes from U-Haul.

He set down the boxes and held up a tape gun. Its metal flap clacked as he waved it around. "We're armed and ready."

"Cute, Dad."

Dakota sat cross-legged on the couch while her parents moved through the house. She wasn't up to following them up and down the stairs, and she had no desire to sit at the little kitchen table in clear view of the basement door. The living room was safer, and the pastry box fit nicely on the coffee table. She worked through half of it, barely stopping to savor the buttery aroma of the cream cheese danishes before stuffing them into her mouth.

Her parents collected depressingly few items to take home with them. Everything from the wake went into the pile of keepsakes, along with some dishes her mother had bought for Lennox, his watch, his framed certificates from various coding programs, and a few knick-knacks that encapsulated Lennox's silly side.

All of it fit into a single box.

"That's it?" Dakota asked over the screeching of the tape gun.

Her father shrugged. "That's it."

Dakota helped them carry the box out to their car and was surprised to find their luggage in the trunk. She looked a question at her father, whose cheeks colored. That was all the answer she needed.

"You're heading back to Tucson," she said flatly. "Already?"

Her father glanced at her mother, and Dakota looked at her—really looked—for the first time that morning. Gaelle's eyes were drawn and tight, and her skin looked ashen, almost like she was coming down with something. Her gaze darted between the house and the car. Dakota had the distinct impression that if a truck backfired or a brick fell off a wall, the sound would spook her mother three feet off the ground.

"You know how much better my health is in a dry climate," Dakota's father said. "We need to get back."

"Yeah, but come on. You spent an entire week here last time we came for Christmas. A few more days won't kill you."

Her mother closed her eyes and shook her head. "Sweetie, I'm exhausted. Last night just wore me out. And today...." Her red eyes locked onto the living room window and she shuddered. "Every minute here feels like a weight around my neck, pulling me down."

Shocked, Dakota stared at her. She'd never heard her mother say anything so dark and dramatic. As Dakota had gotten older, her mother's love for the house had grown. The only reason she'd left it in the first place was because she was forced to choose between it and her husband's health.

Dakota rested her fingertips on her mother's shoulder. "You guys are tired. I get it. But please, there's so much to do here. Can't you just stay?"

"No, we can't," her mother snapped. "Stop pushing this, Dakota. You don't know what we're going through. What we've been through." Clenched fists wobbled at her sides. "Talk to me when you've lost two of your children in the same goddamn house. I can't even stand to *look* at it, and you want me to spend more time here?"

Dakota opened her mouth to tell her she was sorry, but stopped when brimming tears overflowed onto her mother's cheeks.

"I just can't do it." Her mother's voice was quiet now, low and calm. "You have to let me mourn the way I need to."

"Okay." Dakota stepped forward and pulled her mother into a hug. "I get it. You guys go. I've got this."

Her father laid a kiss on top of her head. "We'll do what we can to help from home. We can video chat. Call us if you need help deciding anything."

As her parents drove down the hill, Dakota stared after them, one hand on the porch railing. She kept expecting them to stop, turn around, and come back for her.

They didn't.

Go back inside. You have too much to do to stand out here feeling like an unwanted dog left on the side of the road. And who are you to judge them for abandoning you here? It's no worse than the three of you did to Lennox. Just go inside.

She followed the urge and trudged back through the front door. Her latte, now cold, waited beside the couch. An angry gurgle bubbled up from her stomach. She needed real food before she could start sorting through the rest of Lennox's things, and the leftover pastries wouldn't cut it. Her rental car key glinted from its spot on the hook, and she debated going downtown to grab a sandwich.

Your parents are so exhausting. Just get something delivered. It'll be easier.

With a sigh, she pulled out her phone, ordered takeout, and slumped back onto the couch. She didn't have the energy to leave, no matter how much she wished she could follow her parents to the airport and go back to ignoring the sadness permeating these walls.

Chapter Eleven

Not long after Dakota threw her fish-and-chips wrapper into the garbage, a horn honked outside. Gina was backing her white SUV carefully up the narrow driveway, apparently not fast enough for the minivan that wanted to get around her.

Dakota opened the door and read the vinyl lettering across Gina's back window. REGINA QUEEN OF CLEAN arched above a phone number.

"Hey there!" Gina called as she opened the hatch and pulled out a narrow, five-foot-long duffle.

"Need a hand?"

"Nope. I brought a little helper with me."

The passenger door slammed, and second figure rounded the back of the SUV. The ten-year-old girl was a miniature of Gina, nowhere near her mother's full height but with long, slender limbs that guaranteed she would catch up soon.

Gina nodded at her. "This is my daughter, Allie. You don't mind, do you?"

"No, of course not."

"Thanks. Lennox wouldn't let me bring her. I kind of get it. Not everybody likes kids. But childcare is a bitch."

The way she put it made Dakota laugh. She hadn't had to deal with babysitters or daycare. By the time her mother went back to work, Lennox had been old enough to watch her after school. But it struck her as odd. Lennox had always been a generous person, willing to sacrifice his time and money for everyone he cared about. Allowing Gina to bring Allie while she cleaned would have been a small thing. Why hadn't he been willing to do it?

Gina and Allie carted the cleaning supplies into the living room. Hands on hips, Gina surveyed the space.

"This'll be easy. Two days, maybe three, and the whole place'll be spotless."

"Sounds good. I'll..." Dakota trailed off. She'd caught sight of something on Gina's neck, just barely peeking out above the neckline of her blue smock, and her eyes lit up with glee.

Gina clocked Dakota's expression and yanked her undershirt up higher. "Allie, I think I left my phone in the car. Would you go get it?"

Dakota gave Gina the courtesy of waiting until Allie was outside before bursting into laughter.

"It's not what you think," Gina said quickly.

"Really? Because I think you've got a hickey like a kid at their first make-out party."

A red flush raced up Gina's face.

"Where'd you get it?" Dakota knew she had no right prying into Gina's business. They hadn't been friends in high school, and they weren't really friends now. But they weren't strangers, either. And she would have seized on any opportunity to avoid thinking about the dismal task ahead. "Don't say it was your curling iron. I invented that one."

"Fine. The wake went on for a while after you left last night, and Quinn and I got a little... carried away."

"Quinn? Lennox's friend?"

"Yeah." Gina's blush deepened.

"Are you guys a couple now?"

"I don't know. It's just casual. No labels. Besides, he lives in Texas. It probably won't last once he goes home."

"Shame. He's cute."

"Right?" Gina's eyes danced. "He's a pretty cool guy, too. Smart. He works on video games, like that Haunted-whatever thing Allie's always playing."

Before Dakota could pry any further, the front door slammed. Allie came back inside and shrugged at her mother. "Couldn't find your phone."

"That's okay." Gina winked at Dakota. "I'm sure it'll turn up somewhere. Help me open those curtains. Let's get some light in here."

Dakota blinked. She didn't remember closing the curtains. In fact, she was sure they'd been open before Gina arrived. Hadn't they? No, they had to be. Dakota wouldn't have eaten lunch in a dark living room, hidden from the world outside.

"Do you know where he got those?" Dakota asked Gina as Allie tugged the curtains open. "I could swear he never had any window coverings before."

Gina cracked a smile. "He didn't. Trust me, I'm the one who fielded the neighbors' complaints every week. He was never, uh, fully nude, but for most people, the bar is a lot higher than that."

"Ah. So that's why he put them up."

"No, he didn't care what anybody thought. He said everyone would find a reason to call him weird no matter what he did. But a couple months ago he ordered curtains for all the windows, and I helped him hang them. He said he liked the dark."

Dakota frowned. Lennox had never been comfortable in darkness. She had stopped using a night-light at eleven years old, but unless he'd left it in his bedroom as a decoration, Lennox clearly still used one.

As she stood there trying to puzzle out how Lennox had suddenly gotten over his fear of the dark, Gina got to work in the kitchen, where she announced she would have the oven looking new again in no time. Allie slid onto the couch like an eel and pulled out a handheld video game. The electronic music and pinging sound effects chased

Dakota upstairs to finally start the tedious task of emptying the house.

The problem, she decided, was that she didn't have a deadline. She always functioned best when she was under the gun. If there was nobody breathing down her neck and waiting for her to do something, she would never stop inventing ways to procrastinate.

She paused on the landing and used her phone to find the name of a real estate agency in town. After leaving a voicemail requesting a call back about listing the house, a plan took shape in her mind. She would start with the easiest bedroom: her own.

It had been six years since she graduated from college and landed her job in Atlanta. By then, she'd already taken everything she needed or wanted from this room. Armed with a cardboard box and a black garbage bag, she began ruthlessly sorting the remnants of her childhood into things to donate or things to throw away. Time slipped away as item after item fell to her onslaught. She quickly found a groove, able to focus for the first time without the voice in her head getting in the way.

Just as she finished emptying her old desk, the skin on the back of her neck tingled.

Someone was watching her.

Dakota took a breath and turned her head.

Allie stood at the doorway. Only her face and one hand were visible around the edge. "What are you doing?"

"Packing my old things."

"Are you moving?"

"Sort of. I moved a long time ago. Some of it's going home with me. I'm donating the rest to the thrift store. Want anything?"

"Maybe."

Allie sat on the floor. She picked through books and costume jewelry, going so far as to set a few items aside, but her eyes never stayed away from Dakota for long.

Dakota waited. If the kid had something to ask, she wasn't going to push her. God only knew what it could be.

"Is it true this house is haunted?" Allie asked.

Dakota raised an eyebrow. "Is that what they say?"

"Yeah. Bobby Fredriksen says a mean old witch lives here, and if kids get too close, she eats them."

Of course the children thought that. Lennox had turned himself into a curiosity. The only things the neighborhood children probably saw were lights turning on and off in an otherwise empty house. She couldn't even feel sad about it. If there'd been a house like this nearby while she and Lennox were growing up, they would have thought the same thing.

Well, not after Lennox proved there was no such thing as ghosts. Her feet had been firmly stuck in the real world since then.

Kai, though... Kai was a believer. He never talked about ghosts, never called anything by that name. But the way he talked about the "Whisper Lady" who lived in the basement made her sound more like a malicious phantom than an imaginary friend. He was as scared of her as Dakota was of any on-screen monster. Whether or not he said the word, she knew Kai would think a house as dark and quiet as Lennox's was haunted.

"So is it?" Allie prodded.

"Of course not. Don't listen to kids like that. They're just trying to scare you."

"I guess."

You'll never get anything done with her around. Can't she go play somewhere else?

"Look, I'll just be doing boring stuff up here," Dakota said. "Why don't you go help your mom?"

Allie shrugged. "Okay."

Once the girl was gone, Dakota let out a long sigh and got back to her task. It was satisfying work seeing the way the shelves and walls emptied as she moved through the room.

Before long, the black bag was filled to bursting with old trophy ribbons, posters, saved birthday cards, and the clothes and shoes that were too worn out and ratty to donate. Dakota cinched it closed. Carrying it down the stairs and heaving it into the garbage barrel outside felt like its own reward, but she still decided to treat herself to a Dr

Pepper from the fridge. She cracked the can open and let the cold liquid fizz down her throat.

This would be easy, she decided. Why had she put it off for so long? If she kept up this pace, she could turn the key over to a realtor in a few days and be done with it.

The refrigerator door swung closed with a light thunk. At the same moment, a heavy thud sounded from beneath her feet.

Dakota leaned to the side and peeked at basement door through the kitchen doorway. It was closed, same as she'd left it that morning.

"Gina?" she called.

"Yeah?" Gina's voice was nearby, but echoed thinly.

"Where are you?"

"Scrubbing out the tub."

"Is Allie with you?"

"No, I heard her go out back a few minutes ago. Why?"

Dakota didn't answer. A second thump rumbled through the floorboards from the basement.

Something was down there.

Chapter Twelve

Dakota stood in front of the basement door, clenching her hands into fists and flexing them open over and over.

"Stop being ridiculous," she muttered to herself under her breath. "You're an adult. There's nothing scary down there."

She suddenly remembered a shelf at the far end of the basement. Her mother had kept food storage on it before Kai died. She would disappear down the stairs only to reappear moments later with a jar of canned peaches soaked in sweet syrup. A blue-and-white bag of sugar had sat on that shelf with other supplies, and Dakota could easily picture mice nibbling at its corner and living on it for years. The thump could have been the sound of the bag falling over. Yes, that was all. Just a half-empty sack of sugar tumbling to the floor and leaving a surprised rodent standing on the shelf.

The image of a startled cartoon mouse made her laugh, and her tension dissipated. She was being silly. Going downstairs would be easy.

"Easy," she repeated to herself as she turned the knob.

Cool air breathed out of the open door. The sharp odor of mildew tickled Dakota's nose and made her sneeze. It took her a moment to remember which side of the door the light switch was on, and when her hand found it, it was already flipped up. A wave of panic washed over her. She remembered the morning she'd heard about Lennox, the burned-out bulb in her bathroom, the silver eyes above the shower. That was what waited for her below. She could feel it. If she took a single step forward, the glowing-eyed thing would reach one bony hand through the empty back of the stairs and grab her ankle.

Dakota knew what would happen then. She'd seen it a thousand times in her nightmares. Like Kai, she would tumble down the stairs to her death.

Something thudded to the floor below. "Whoops."

The voice pierced through the cloud of fear surrounding Dakota. It didn't belong to a monster.

"Allie?" she called.

"Yeah?"

The flood of relief powered Dakota downstairs like a waterslide. She found Allie at the bottom, rummaging through a shelf of picture books and baby supplies.

"What are you doing down here?" Dakota asked.

"I thought I heard somebody talking."

"So you just came down here by yourself? What if it was someone dangerous who isn't supposed to be here?"

Allie shrugged. "They didn't sound dangerous. It sounded like a little boy. But there's nobody down here. I looked. I think it was just the furnace"

Dakota stared at the girl. It had taken Dakota several whole minutes to work up the courage to walk down the stairs, and Allie had just waltzed down them and poked around down here?

"You're pretty brave," she said. "Some people might think this place is spooky."

"It's just a basement." Allie looked around, her young face filled with curiosity. "Did you live down here?"

"No. Nobody did."

"Why not?"

Dakota hesitated. How could she explain it to a child? Why her parents stopped coming down here, why they moved the washer and dryer upstairs, why the door stood firmly closed until the family almost forgot it was there?

It wasn't supposed to be that way. Even before they adopted Lennox, her parents had a vision of what their life would be. Their plan was to build five bedrooms and a playroom in the basement, which would give them room to adopt or foster more children like Lennox, Dakota, and Kai—children who needed a home. They saw a big family, ever growing, with more children moving in when the older ones moved out.

Then Kai died.

At first, Dakota didn't understand it. She thought they would eventually finish the framed-in walls and put in carpet. She thought she and Lennox would move down here, making room for the younger kids to be nearer to her parents. But her mother folded in on herself. She declared she couldn't stand being trapped in the house, found a job, and threw herself into the work. Her father did the same. They left Lennox to look after Dakota in the afternoons, and until her parents finally crawled out of their cocoons of grief, he was the one she ran to when terror woke her in the middle of the night.

Allie was watching Dakota intently, still waiting for an answer to her question.

Dakota sighed. "Because sometimes life doesn't go the way you want. Come on, let's go upstairs."

"Wait." Allie crouched down beside the bookshelf. When she stood, a familiar white box was in her hands.

Mouse Trap.

Dakota's eyes widened. "Where did you find that?"

"Right here. There's a bunch of games. Can we play one?"

"Sure." Dakota took Mouse Trap from Allie. "Uh, but not this one. It's missing some pieces. Is Trouble over there?"

"Yeah."

"Grab that one. You'll like the dice popper. It's fun."

Allie obediently picked Trouble out of the dusty pile of board games and scampered up the stairs. Dakota tucked Mouse Trap under her arm and started to follow her.

A tingle ran up her neck. Someone was watching her, and this time, she knew it couldn't be Allie.

Swallowing, she slowly turned around. The uncovered bulb above her bathed most of the basement in light, but shadows lingered at the edges of the room. She searched them for anything or anyone that didn't belong. Her gaze landed on a support beam not far from the door to the concrete stairs outside.

Something dark was wrapped around it.

Long and thin, the hazy shape ended in a point. Dakota squinted and leaned forward. It almost looked like a skinny caterpillar. But as she watched, it bent, crooking toward her like a finger, beckoning her forward.

Gooseflesh erupted over Dakota's body as every hair on her arms lifted away from her skin. A forgotten feeling rose up in her. The knowledge, the incontestable fact that something foul and malignant hid in the darkness, filled her so quickly that she retched. Nothing came out of her mouth. It lingered there, choking her.

As a scream struggled to break past the blockage, Dakota bolted after Allie.

Chapter Thirteen

The entire time she and Allie were playing Trouble, Dakota glanced back and forth between the game and the closed basement door. Each pop of the dome-covered dice made her jump, and she was so distracted that she couldn't follow the simple gameplay.

Allie raised her arms in a V. "I won!"

"Good job," Dakota said. Allie could have cheated her way to victory and Dakota never would have noticed.

When the pieces were packed back into their box, Allie watched TV while Dakota stared at a spot of nothing at the wall. She kept seeing the pointed finger on the post, inviting her to come closer and lose herself in the darkness.

It was nothing. You're just being a coward. Grow up, Dakota.

That was the problem, she decided. Being here made her feel like she was eight years old again, frightened by every shadow. The house had turned her back into a scared little girl.

There's nothing to be afraid of. You know you're safer here than anywhere else in the world.

Allie muted the television when Gina hauled her supplies in from Lennox's room. "Are we going home soon?"

"Yep. I'm done with the main floor." Gina turned her attention to Dakota. "I take weekends off, but I'll be back on Monday to clean upstairs."

"That sounds great," Dakota said.

"I'll tackle the basement last."

"The basement?" Even the word made Dakota's pulse race. She couldn't go back down there. Nothing and no one could make her. "Right. Yeah."

"You okay?" Gina asked.

Dakota lied out of instinct, programmed by society to answer any question about her wellbeing the same way. "I'm fine."

Gina frowned. "If you say so. I'll see you Monday, okay?"

"Thanks. I really appreciate it."

The house felt too quiet without the whirr of Gina's vacuum cleaner or Allie's beeping video game. But Dakota was relieved they were gone. She hadn't realized until they left how much their presence strained her. Her body felt tired, as though she'd spent the afternoon pushing against an enormous weight.

But no amount of exhaustion could stop her from retrieving Mouse Trap from the shelf where she'd left it and setting it on the coffee table. She smiled down at the familiar artwork of the elaborate Rube Goldberg machine on the front of the box. She might not have anyone to play with, but she could still build the winding mechanism and send the marble through the chain reaction. That was one piece of her childhood she wouldn't mind reliving.

First, though, she had to satisfy the curiosity that had nearly sent her into the basement that morning. She lifted the lid off the box and flipped it over.

Just like in her dream, black writing covered the inside of the lid. Dakota leaned away from the table and waved her hand in front of her face. The heady stench of the king-size permanent marker was as strong as the day Lennox had used it, and the scent brought back a flood of memory.

She had woken him that night by tugging on the edge of his Transformers blanket.

"Bad dream?" he asked.

"I wasn't sleeping. She's here again."

Lennox sighed. It was a wearier sound than most four-teen-year-olds made, but he carried a heavier burden than most boys his age.

"I know it didn't feel like a dream, but that's what it was," he said. "She isn't real. It's just your imagination."

"No." Dakota's voice was emphatic. Defiant. "She's real. I saw her outside my window."

"How could somebody be outside your window? It's too high."

"She can fly. She was looking at me. Can't you make her go away?"

"Okay, fine. Let's go check."

She looked away as he pushed her bedroom door open all the way. He didn't believe her, but she knew the Whisper Lady would be watching her from the window, hovering there like an owl with round, silver eyes.

"You can look now," Lennox told her. "She's not out there."

Dakota was unconvinced. "What if she came inside while I was in your room?"

Lennox obliged by checking under the bed. Finding nothing, he moved on to the closet. She flinched as he pulled open the accordion doors. Hangers clacked softly together as he moved her clothes around and made an exaggerated show of peering into the corners.

"Told you," he said. "There's nobody here."

"But I heard my name. She told me to come find her. It's the Whisper Lady. The one Kai told me about." Fear gripped Dakota's ribcage and squeezed her voice into a high, thin wail. "She got him, and she's going to get me, too."

"Okay, it's okay." Lennox made calming, shushing sounds and hugged his little sister tightly around her shoulders. "The Whisper Lady can't hurt you. Know how I know?"

Trembling, Dakota shook her head.

"Because ghosts aren't real. They're made up for the movies. Mom and Dad told me so. And they wouldn't lie, right?"

Dakota hesitated. No, her parents would never lie. But even at eight, she sensed a critical difference between lying and simply being wrong. Her parents had been wrong before. They could be wrong about this, too.

Lennox watched her. When she didn't nod or agree with him, he tilted his head and stared up at the ceiling. "Okay, how about I prove it to you?"

"How?"

"Rena Margolis had a game at her birthday party last summer. It's supposed to talk to ghosts. Everybody was all scared, but I could tell Rena was moving the little triangle thing around and trying to freak us out. You and me can play it, and I'll show you there's nothing to be afraid of. Deal?"

Her mind had stuck on the phrase *talk to ghosts*, and she didn't see how any of this was supposed to make her feel better. But Lennox always knew what to do. She put her hand into his and let him lead her out of the room. On tiptoe, they passed the open door to Kai's shrine-like bedroom and crept down the stairs.

Mouse Trap was already on the coffee table, the contraption still set up from their game that afternoon. Lennox ducked into the kitchen and retrieved their father's toolbox from a cupboard.

"We're not supposed to play with that," she whispered. Getting out of bed was one thing, but getting into the toolbox was a groundable offense.

"It's okay. I'll put it back."

He carefully opened it, then paused, staring down the hall toward their parents' bedroom. Nothing moved. Nobody made a sound. He let out a breath, picked a fat black permanent marker out of the collection of tools, and handed it to Dakota. She gripped the cold cylinder in her hands while he put the toolbox back. When he returned, he collected the colorful lid from the Mouse Trap game. After a moment's thought, he grabbed the little blue plastic cage that always clattered to down to trap the mouse and end the game. With a crooked finger, he motioned for Dakota to follow him back upstairs.

They spread their supplies out on Lennox's bedroom floor. The marker's bitter stench made Dakota's eyes water, and she couldn't believe Lennox had it in him to use it for as long as he did. It felt like it took ages for him to write the alphabet on the inside of the box in thick, blocky letters. In the top corners, he wrote "Yes" and "No." When he finished, he capped the marker and put the makeshift board between them.

He held up the Mouse Trap cage. "I forget what this is called, but ghosts are supposed to be able to move this thing around and spell out a message. We'll just put it on top of the letters. How about the W for Whisper Lady?"

Dakota shivered but nodded her approval. It made sense to start there.

"Okay, put your fingers on it like this. No, hold it lighter. Don't push on it. If there's something here, it'll move on its own."

The thought made Dakota's body lock up. She couldn't move the planchette even if she wanted to.

"Ready?" Lennox asked.

She swallowed. No, she wasn't ready. She would never be ready to talk to a ghost. But Lennox's encouraging smile made her feel ten percent braver that she really was, and she gave him another single, quick nod.

"Great. I'll ask the questions." Lennox straightened his spine and closed his eyes. "Hi, ghosts. You have five minutes to prove you exist."

He peeked one eye open and made a show of looking around the room with a frown on his face.

"See?" he whispered to Dakota. "There's nothing here."

"Ask about the Whisper Lady," she prompted.

Lennox closed his eyes again. "Is there a ghost called the Whisper Lady? If you're there, we want to talk to you."

Dakota didn't even dare to blink. She looked from the board to Lennox's face to every shadow in his bedroom and back again. She was frozen, somehow as terrified of something answering Lennox's questions as she was of nothing happening at all.

"Maybe she can't hear you," she said.

"If she's in the house, she can hear us." He raised his voice slightly, still keeping it quiet enough to avoid waking their parents. "Whisper Lady, if you're real, move the trap.... Now!"

The cool plastic cage stayed utterly still beneath Dakota's fingers.

"See?" Lennox asked. "There's nothing out there. No ghosts. No monsters. Nothing to be afraid of. But you know what? Even if there was, I promise I'll protect you. I'll get right between you and anything that wants to hurt you and stop them from getting you."

"Promise?"

"Pinkie swear."

They each lifted one hand from the plastic cage and hooked their pinkies together. Dakota's chest relaxed. She believed in Lennox. He would do anything to protect her. As long as he was near, nothing could hurt her.

The memory calmed Dakota's nerves. She hadn't seen or heard anything in the shadows after that, and she took comfort in the reminder that Lennox was right. He'd always been right. Ghosts weren't real. The "Whisper Lady" was just a figment of Kai's imagination, and Dakota's young mind had seized on it as a way for her to process his death.

And now you're doing it again. Imagining things. Letting your paranoia run wild with these foolish stories.

Deep down, she knew she wasn't processing Lennox's death. She could feel the grief moving just beneath the surface, like a shark circling below the waves. Eventually, it would burst out of the water and devour her whole.

At some point though, she needed to do it. She had no doubt she would feel better afterward. Less plugged up. There had been an almost unbearable period of darkness in the house after Kai died, a smothering layer of suffering that blocked out everything else. Her parents slept a lot. Dinners were silent except for the scratch of silverware across Corel. Dakota's nightmares were constant, and for nearly a year, everyone in the Scott family existed as pale reflections of their former selves.

She remembered it getting better after the night Lennox had turned the Mouse Trap game into something more important. Her nightmares, while still present, were less frequent. Dinnertime conversations resumed. Her parents' moods grew lighter. Not the same as before, nowhere even near it. But to Dakota's young eyes, her mother and father came back from the dead and started paying attention to their living children again.

The only lingering darkness in the house surrounded Lennox. It was as though he hadn't been able to start mourning until the rest of the family began to heal. Then he turned inward, retreating into himself until he couldn't stand to leave the house.

Dakota straightened her shoulders. That wouldn't happen to her. She would only shove her pain aside as long as it took to take care of things here. Then, when she was back in Atlanta with the sale of Lennox's house behind her, she could properly grieve.

She didn't register the way her subconscious was already working overtime to fold her sorrow into a neat little parcel that would ultimately be stored beside every other unwanted emotion.

All of this is wearing you out. Wouldn't it be easier to just stay in Astoria? You could live here the way you did as a child.

Dakota sank down onto the couch. She did feel comfortable here. Lennox's memory was all around her. Protecting her. It added to the home's intrinsic charms, with its high ceilings and arched doorways.

Keep the house. Lennox would have wanted it that way. Why else would he leave it to you?

The idea's appeal grew. Lennox had already paid off the house. She wouldn't have to worry about rent. He had left her a life-changing gift.

Lennox was always your protector. Maybe he knew something you didn't. He knew how safe it is here. How perfect your life could be if you came back for good.

Her ties to Georgia suddenly seemed weak and superficial. She was already making friends in Astoria again. Why not stay?

She was too tired to make any decisions, but she promised herself she would give it some serious thought later. For now, she lay down, head on the armrest and feet on the cushions, and stared at the muted television as the curtains inched closed behind her.

Chapter Fourteen

A frantic pounding on the door woke Dakota. She peeled her cheek away from the damp upholstery and blinked around the dark room. She felt groggy and sleep logged, like she'd taken too long of a nap.

"Dakota?" Gina called from outside. "Dakota, open up."

"Coming," Dakota croaked. Her joints popped as she stood, and she yawned widely.

Gina's features sagged in relief when Dakota opened the door. "Jesus Christ, you scared the hell out of me. I've been banging on the door for like five minutes. I was starting worry I was about to find you the way..."

She trailed off, but Dakota filled in the blank. The way she had found Lennox's body when she got there to clean. Dakota hadn't realized Gina was so melodramatic.

"Sorry. I fell asleep after you guys finished up. I didn't think you'd be back so soon."

"Soon?" Gina arched an eyebrow. "Have you been asleep this whole time? It's been, like, a solid day since we left."

Her words were slow to penetrate Dakota's sleepy mind. "Really?"

Gina put her palm on Dakota's forehead. "Do you feel sick?"

"No, just tired."

"Good. Know what'll help with that?"

Another nap. Go back to sleep.

"No, what?" Dakota stifled another yawn.

"Getting you out of the house and doing something fun. Come on." Gina marched across the room and yanked open the curtains.

Dakota squinted against the late afternoon sunlight. Was it possible she'd really slept that long? She lifted one arm and took a tentative sniff of her armpit. Yep. It'd been at least a day since she'd showered.

"What'd you have in mind?" she asked.

"Let's start with dinner. Hungry, Rip Van Winkle?"

Dakota's stomach squeaked in answer.

Gina laughed. "Good, because I'm starving. You go get cleaned up. I'll call Quinn and figure out where we're going."

You should just stay home. Order a pizza. It would be so much easier.

The temptation toward sloth couldn't compete with Gina's determination to drag Dakota to dinner, and Dakota allowed herself to be chased upstairs and into the shower. The hot water finished the job the sunlight had started, and by the time she was dry, Dakota had come around to Gina's line of thinking. She'd been inside these walls for too long. It was time to stretch her legs. And even more importantly, time to get some food that wasn't deep fried.

It was warm enough outside for knee shorts and a thin hoodie. Pulling on bright-colored clothes made her feel like herself again, and she whistled as she flipped light switches on her way down the stairs.

A second spotlight had gone out in the living room. She promised to remind herself to pick up some replacement bulbs on the way home from dinner.

"Ready?" Gina asked.

"Yeah, want me to drive?"

"No way. I'm your designated driver tonight. I saw you sipping that soda at the wake." Gina flashed her a grin and pulled open the front door. "If you wanna burn off a shitty week, you gotta get lit."

Just as they were stepping outside, Gina grabbed Dakota's wrist and stopped her from turning off the lights. Dakota raised an eyebrow at her.

"Sorry," Gina said, pulling her hand back sheepishly. "Old habit. Lennox always used to leave the lights on. I feel like...." She trailed off, and the edge of her lower lip wobbled between her teeth as she searched for the right words. "When Allie was little, we had this cat. He was already pretty old when we adopted him, and he only lasted a few years with us before he got sick. At the end, he was always looking for somewhere to hide, like he wanted to crawl inside a dark hole and fade away. Looking back, I can't shake this feeling that Lennox was doing the same thing. Only he couldn't go find somewhere to hide without leaving the house, so he made his own dark hole right here. And I wish...." She looked away. "I wish I'd figured that out sooner. Maybe I could have, I don't know, helped him."

Dakota didn't tell Gina that she'd been having similar thoughts. That if she'd paid attention to the right things, noticed the way Lennox was changing, she would have realized that something was horribly wrong. But she couldn't say those things aloud. She couldn't risk the grief and the guilt breaking out of the careful boxes into which she'd packed them, especially not in front of an audience.

"It's okay," she said at last. "Let's leave the lights on. It'll remind me to change a couple of burned-out bulbs later."

Whether it was out of some self-imposed penance or a genuine interest in Dakota's needs, Gina insisted they stop at the hardware store on the way to the restaurant for spotlight bulbs to be sure they didn't forget after dinner. Or, as she put it, after their night-long, back-in-time, we're-still-young evening on the town.

Quinn was waiting for them outside the restaurant. The light summer breeze lofted a few of his dark curls into the air, and an excited smile spread across his face when he caught sight of Gina.

"You sure you want me crashing your party?" Dakota whispered.

"Positive." Gina gave her a quick wink. "I'm as excited to hang out with you as I am with him."

When they reached Quinn, he bowed low with one hand behind his back. "Ladies. So good of you to join me."

Gina giggled, and Quinn's charms and energy weren't lost on Dakota, either. Her spirits immediately lifted as she followed the "no labels" couple to their table. Or it might have been the aromas of freshly grilled seafood and hoppy beer swirling around the restaurant. Either way, she was glad she came.

By the time the waitress had finished taking their order, Dakota had already finished her initial assessment of Quinn. He was endearingly goofy. He was completely smitten by Gina.

And he was a chatterbox.

"Have you guys seen those big ships on the river?" he asked, as though there was any possibility they hadn't. "It's crazy. I thought those things were just for the ocean.

They're totally loaded with cargo containers, too. I can't even imagine how much stuff is on those things."

He seemed interested in and excited by everything around him. The river, the mild climate, the city's cinematic history—all of it had been background noise to Dakota before, just an ordinary part of living here. But Quinn's enthusiasm was contagious, and she began to see some of the town's history through his eyes.

"Lennox didn't do this place justice," he said. "He talked about how much he loved living here and how good the food is, but I mean everybody talks like that about their hometown. Lennox is actually right about his."

Hearing her brother's name come out of such a positive person's mouth made Dakota smile.

"Did you guys talk a lot?" she asked.

"Oh yeah, all the time. We had raids three, sometimes four times a week. You game?"

"Game for what?" she said, misunderstanding the question.

"No, I mean do you play any MMOs? Like did you play with Lennox?"

She shook her head. "Just board games."

"Oh man, I love board games! We should play some while we're both still here. When do you go home?"

Their food and cocktails arrived, giving Dakota time to consider his question. She mentally ping-ponged back and forth between her options. Until yesterday, she hadn't really considered staying, but all of Quinn's gushing was adding to that side of the scales. She suspected the decision would come down to which one was more work: selling Lennox's house, or moving all her stuff from Atlanta to Astoria.

Eventually, she settled on, "It depends on how things go with the house. How long are you in town?"

Quinn glanced at Gina, and a pink tinge crept into his cheeks. "I don't know. There's something about this place. It sounds crazy, but I've been looking at property since I got here."

"Want to buy mine?" Dakota asked, only half joking.

"Don't make that offer to Allie," Gina said. "She's already obsessed with your house. Or maybe it's with you. She's been hassling me all day. She keeps telling me, 'I want to play in the basement with that lady.'"

Dakota smiled. "Well, I don't want to hang out in the basement, but she's welcome to come over and play board games any time."

"I'm going to take you up on that. You've been warned." Gina turned to Quinn and asked, almost casually, "Is moving here something you would really do? Could you keep your job?"

"Oh, for sure. I can write anywhere." He swallowed a pink piece of salmon. "I work from home half the time anyway, just so I don't have to put on real pants."

Dakota furrowed her brow. "You're a writer? I thought Gina said you make video games."

"Yeah, I do. Well, I don't *make* them, make them. I'm not a coder or anything. I write the story. You know, develop the narrative, create monster backgrounds, write the character dialogue, all that stuff. Actually, it might be kind of cool to live somewhere different for a while. Pull some of the local flavor into the games. Are there any urban legends around here? Ghosts or cryptids, anything like that?"

"I don't know what a cryptid is," Gina said, "but all of Allie's classmates think Dakota's house is haunted."

"Really? Hang on." Quinn nudged his plate to the side, making room for a small notebook from his jacket pocket. "Tell me *everything*."

Chapter Fifteen

"First things first." Quinn clicked his pen open and hovered the tip above a blank page. "Is the house haunted by ghosts or demons?"

Gina laughed. "You sound like you believe those kids. They're ten, Quinn."

"That doesn't mean they're not right. I did a ton of research for our last game, *Haunted Hellevision.* A bunch of parapsychologists did this big study, and they figured out that kids can see stuff adults can't. It's like we lose a sense as we get older. Isn't that crazy? It'd be like if you slowly stopped being able to see the color blue between, like, eight and twelve."

Dakota stiffened. "Why those ages?"

"I wasn't trying to be specific or anything. I figure it would be different for everybody, like when you lose your baby teeth."

Gina tapped the edge of Dakota's half-empty stein of beer. "Are you drunk? Don't tell me you're freaked out by this stuff."

"I'm not," Dakota said quickly, hoping to mask the trickle of unease that was creeping up the back of her neck like a single, teasing fingernail. "Not anymore, anyway. It's just interesting. I was eight when Lennox finally convinced me I didn't have to be afraid of the dark. I'm just curious, that's all. It's not everyday you go to dinner and somebody starts talking about demons."

"Yeah, would you explain that, please?" Gina asked Quinn. "You said 'ghosts or demons.' Are they different?"

"Well, yeah." Quinn looked at her as though the answer was obvious. When she didn't say anything, he shrugged. "Ghosts were human once. They have human wants and needs that are connected to their human lives. Once those needs are met, they can move on, like meeting a game's objectives and moving up to the next level. But demons were never human. There's nothing waiting for them after this. Their appetites are inhuman, and they'll never be satisfied enough to stop going after the things they want."

The things they want. The words bumped the trickle on Dakota's neck up to a firehose. It felt like a dinner fork dragged up her skin and into her hair, where it tangled and tugged at her scalp.

"She wants me to find her."

Kai had said it.

And so had she.

"What do they want?" she asked, voice barely more than a whisper.

Even over the clatter of silverware on plates and the hum of voices from surrounding tables, Quinn heard her. His eyes flashed, and a wicked smile crept over his face, as though he was enjoying the chance to frighten someone with his wealth of supernatural knowledge.

"It depends. They might be guardians who want to keep humans away from sacred places. Or they could be vengeful spirits, determined to punish innocent people over some ancient beef. Maybe they want to gorge themselves on our negative emotions. Anger, jealousy, grief, guilt—the stronger, the better. Or maybe they're just aimless, malevolent beings with a destructive streak. That's why I love writing them into our games. There's no limit to their evil."

Gina tapped the table. "I think we all need a drink after that."

She ordered another round, staying true to her promise to be the designated driver while simultaneously encouraging the others to upgrade from regular beers to boilermakers. The conversation at their table meandered from topic to topic while steadily growing louder. But no matter what Gina and Quinn talked about, Dakota's mind strayed back to Quinn's demonic theories. She wasn't sure if he really believed in any of it, or if he was simply a collector of game-worthy lore and a gleeful campfire storyteller.

As glass after glass disappeared, she thought about asking him. But every time she did, her mind filled with a vision of that single, claw-like finger beckoning to her across the basement while Allie's footsteps thundered up the stairs. So instead, she kept her mouth shut.

Before long, she was sliding down the puffy back of their booth and struggling to focus on what the others were saying. She blinked slowly. Keeping her eyes open was even harder than processing the conversation.

"Okay," Gina said as Dakota slumped to the side. "Let's get our lightweight home."

Whether it was the alcohol, the amount of food, or simply the toll the past week had taken on her, Dakota thought she might fall asleep on her feet. She leaned heavily against Gina as they made their way back to the car. The crisp air sobered her up a fraction of an inch, but she still felt woozy and unstable.

Quinn rubbed an eyebrow and squinted down the street. "I think I overdid it, too. Can you give me a ride?"

"For sure," Gina said. "Mind if we drop her off first?"

Once she was buckled in, Dakota leaned her forehead against the cool glass. They'd been talking about something earlier, something that had seemed so important at the time, but she couldn't remember what it was now. She only remembered echoing laughter and the citrus tang of the beer. She felt fully relaxed, and her limbs melted into the faux leather upholstery.

Gina parked in the driveway, and Quinn helped Dakota out of the car. They were halfway up the walk to the house with Dakota's arms slung around each of their shoulders when Gina stopped and stared at the front window.

"Didn't we leave the lights on?" she asked.

Dakota squinted at the house. Its edges swam, but she registered the curtains had been drawn and no light shone through the edges. "Muss not've," she slurred, pulling forward.

Gina didn't move. "No, we definitely did. We talked about it. You bought lightbulbs—dammit, they're still in my car."

A thin tendril of shadow flitted beneath the door and embraced Dakota around the waist.

You don't need any more lights. You're more comfortable in the dark.

Dakota's abdomen contracted. She clapped a hand over her mouth and fell to her knees beside the steps. Fish, beer, and one too many shots of whiskey splattered onto the walk. Body shuddering, she gasped in air and exhaled vomit until her stomach was empty.

She felt Gina's hands on her back and shot her a watery, apologetic smile. "Sorry. God, I'm gross."

"Shh, it's okay." Gina moved her hand in circles between Dakota's shoulder blades. "I'm a mom. Nothing grosses me out anymore." After a minute, she asked, "Think you can go inside?"

Dakota nodded shakily. The others helped her into the house, up the stairs, and into her bedroom. Gina slipped the shoes off Dakota's feet while Quinn got her a glass of water from the kitchen. At Gina's insistence, Dakota sipped it slowly.

Gina's phone pinged. "Balls. I told Allie's sitter I'd be home by ten." She studied Dakota with concern. "If I had anywhere to put her, I'd take her with me."

"I'll stay," Quinn volunteered. "I can sleep on the couch."

"You'd do that?"

He leaned forward and squeezed Gina's hand. "For sure. It's no problem."

"You could have Lennox's bed. I'll make it up with clean sheets."

Quinn recoiled, pulling away from her. "As much as I love spooky shit, I'll be way more comfortable on the couch than in my dead friend's bed."

Gina glanced out into the hallway and lowered her voice. "When she's settled, will you help me check the house real quick? I know it's nothing, but those curtains...."

"Yeah," Quinn said. "Of course."

Once Dakota finished the water, Gina tucked her under a blanket. She clicked on the soccer ball-shaped bedside lamp and rested a hand on Dakota's forehead.

"Quinn'll be right downstairs, okay? Call him if you need anything."

"Okay," Dakota said sleepily. She felt like a little girl again, getting put to bed after a long day. Reality and memory fuzzed together. She imagined she heard the music of a late-night talk show playing on the television downstairs and her father's staccato laughter as her parents shared a nightcap the way they'd done before Kai died.

It was better back then. Your whole family under one roof. Why did you wait until Lennox was gone to think about moving back here? If you had done it sooner, he would still be alive.

Dakota let out a long, low coo of regret that almost sounded like a snore. Gina and Quinn left her, switching off the overhead light and leaving her door cracked a few inches. Their whispered conversation faded away as they peeked into the other bedrooms and tiptoed down the stairs to the living room.

As their feet reached the last step, the bulb in Dakota's lamp flickered and burned out.

Chapter Sixteen

D akota began the next day with a gravely moan. Everything hurt, even her throat. She peeked one eye open to check the time, then lay back and flung an arm over her face.

The night before ran through her mind in disjointed pieces, like someone had gouged chunks out of her memory with a heavy pair of kitchen scissors. She remembered being in the restaurant. The din and the energy had been exhilarating. She saw Quinn's mischievous grin, Gina laughing, then—

She could still taste the next part. Lingering traces of vomit coated the back of her teeth. A question—*Does she clean the outside of the house too?*—flitted briefly through her mind before she shut it down. Dakota wouldn't ask Gina to do that. It was too foul. She would hose the walk off herself just as soon as she managed to claw her way out of bed.

It took longer than usual. Even the day after a hockey or kickball game, when her muscles burned and her stomach roiled from the post-match celebration, it didn't take her more than a few minutes to muster the energy required to hunt down a cup of coffee. But on those mornings, it was euphoria that clung to her psyche, not shame and regret.

Great job mourning you're doing. That's exactly how Lennox would want you to honor his memory. Puking in his garden and letting a stranger shack up in his house. You're a disgrace.

She found Quinn passed out on the couch downstairs, facedown with one leg hanging off the cushions. A Sunday morning service was on TV, audio turned down low. She bent and shook his shoulder gently.

Quinn screamed and jerked upright, blinking around the room in a panic.

Dakota put up her hands. "Whoa, sorry. It's okay. It's just me."

His frantic eyes calmed, but it took time for his heavy breathing to slow and his muscles to relax. When he finally sat back against the cushions, his face was sheepish. He dragged a hand from his forehead to his chin.

"Shit, sorry," he said. "I, uh... I think I was having a nightmare."

"Don't apologize. I get it."

As terrible as Dakota felt, Quinn looked worse. His skin was clammy, and his lips were chapped and raw, as though he'd just panted his way through a half marathon.

A muscle beneath his eye twitched as he gazed into the dark corners of the room with suspicion.

She threw open the curtains and turned on the lights. A third spotlight was out now. Gina had thoughtfully left the bag of bulbs on the kitchen counter, and Dakota got to work swapping them out while Quinn went to the bathroom.

"You okay?" she asked when he emerged.

"Yeah, fine." He managed a weak smile. "The perils of having a vivid imagination. Sometimes it gets away from me."

For a moment, he didn't say anything more. But just as Dakota was wondering if he was less chatty when he was sober, a cascade of words tumbled out of his mouth.

"Did you ever think this house might really be haunted? Not the way the kids in Allie's class think, you know, where anyplace with no lights on is spooky by default. I mean, did you ever feel anything here?" He looked at her, and she wasn't sure whether he was hoping for a yes or a no. "Or did Lennox?"

"Lennox didn't believe in ghosts."

"Do you?"

The question floated in the air above them, mingling with the scattered particles of dust drifting in the sunlight.

"I used to," she said at last. "Before Lennox proved me wrong."

"Kind of hard to prove a negative."

His words were sharp, more staccato than she'd grown to expect. The change in his demeanor startled her. He met her gaze, and snippets of their conversation the night before came back to her. She remembered him asking about ghosts and demons, but his face was far more serious now than it had been in the restaurant.

"You actually believe it all, don't you?" she asked. "The stuff you write about in your games."

"Just the pieces I find outside my mind," he answered softly.

"Maybe this will help. I'll show you how Lennox chased my fears away for good."

She crossed the room and pulled Mouse Trap off the shelf, ignoring the amusement that played at the edges of Quinn's lips as she set the game onto the coffee table.

His smile faded when she lifted the lid. He yanked it out of her hands and slammed it back over the game.

"Is that a Ouija board?" he demanded, jerking his hands away from the box as though it had burned him.

"Yeah, Lennox made it."

Quinn's eyes bulged. "He *made* it?"

The horror in his voice only strengthened her resolve.

"I can see that you're scared," she said. "But just trust me. You believe in ghosts, right? And that you can talk to them with a Ouija board?"

He gave her a single, terse nod.

"Okay. And it seems like you also think this house is haunted."

"Well, if it wasn't before, it will be now." He looked genuinely angry. "You can't screw around with this shit, Dakota. I know Parker Brothers sold them as toys, but spirit boards were a thing way before they started advertising them to kids. The guy who manufactured them got lots of ideas from one of these things. It told him to build a factory, and guess what? He died falling off that same factory's roof a few years later. What if the idea to market them as games came from a board, too, huh? What if whatever's haunting your house gave Lennox the idea to make one?"

His rapid-fire delivery made Dakota feel out of breath. She breathed in deeply before hitting him with a succinct counterargument. "If you're so sure these things work, just try it with me. You'll see that I'm right."

They sat there for a while, locked in a staring contest over the multicolored Mouse Trap cover. Dakota didn't stop to ask herself why it was so important to her that she prove him wrong about the house being haunted. She just leaned into the polished wood table and forced all of her will into her glare.

He blinked, and Dakota sat back in triumph. But Quinn hadn't given in.

With a shake of his head, he got to his feet and collected his jacket. "I need to get out of here. I'm exhausted, I slept like shit, and I smell like a rhino's butt. Will you drive me to my hotel?"

Dakota sighed. "Sure."

They drove in silence, windshield wipers squeaking back and forth against the light morning drizzle. The smell of rain cleared Dakota's head, and before they'd even gotten downtown, she felt like a bully.

"I'm sorry for being a jackass," she said. "I shouldn't have pushed you like that."

Quinn shook his head. "I'm sorry, too. I shouldn't have been talking about ghosts at dinner, and I shouldn't have brought it up again today. Not after Gina told me what happened to your little brother."

She was surprised he hadn't already known about Kai. "Lennox never mentioned it?"

"No. But we usually kept it pretty light in the chat, you know? Just bullshitting about music or shows or whatever while we waited for all the slowpokes to join the raid. If I'd known...." He paused. "Actually, no. I wouldn't have done anything different if I'd known. If Lennox wanted to talk to somebody about it, it probably would have been to you."

Dakota pursed her lips. She and Lennox rarely talked about Kai. If they did, it was to share happy memories. They talked about the things Kai loved—backyard games, Candyland, goofy kids' shows with felt puppets.

They never discussed their grief. And despite her gentle probing, they never explored the reasons why Lennox stopped going outside.

Why didn't you push it more? You could have helped him.

Tears brimmed in the corners of her eyes as they pulled up to the hotel. She blinked them back and stared out the windshield.

Quinn unbuckled his seat belt. He hesitated before stepping out of the car. "Promise me you won't use that board. Bury it, burn it, whatever you have to do to make sure you don't use it."

Dakota forced a laugh and held up a hand like she was taking a courtroom oath. "I promise."

He searched her eyes and shook his head. "I don't believe you. If you do use it, just don't use it alone, okay? You don't have to promise. You don't even have to listen. Just.... Be careful."

With that, he hopped out of the car and sprinted through the rain. She watched him disappear through the front doors. There was zero chance he would ever come over again. He wouldn't want to see her or have anything to do with her. The realization made her chest hurt. By chasing away her brother's closest friend, she suddenly felt like she had banished the last echo of Lennox's presence in her life.

Chapter Seventeen

Dakota flip-flopped on what to do about Lennox's house all the way home. There were moments where it felt like hers, where she could see herself waking up every day and living her life there. It felt that way when she got back from dropping Quinn off. She strolled right into the kitchen like she owned the place. Which, she thought with a smile, she did. It was no surprise to find the coffee and filters in the same cupboard her mother had kept them. Lennox hadn't rearranged anything after their parents moved to Arizona. Everything in the drawers was exactly where it'd been while she was growing up, down to the tiniest measuring spoon.

If she wanted, she could turn back the clock as far as it would go. It wouldn't be exactly the same without Lennox, but....

No. He was the only thing that had ever drawn her back here. The moment she recognized that, the last waffling tremors of indecision fell away. She would sell the house. Lennox's memory wasn't tied to these walls or even to his possessions. She'd been foolish to think she needed to stay here for his sake. He would want her to do whatever made her happy, even if it meant selling his home and everything in it. Besides, if she was going to uproot everything she'd built in Georgia, it would be to live near her parents in Tucson.

As the thought entered her mind, a dry chill swirled through the kitchen and nipped at her ankles. The cold twisted around her, driving shivers up her body as it cupped her ears.

If you won't stay here, go be with your parents. You could live with them while you find a home of your own. Your mother has missed you so much. She's already lost two children. You're all she has left.

The idea made Dakota giddy. The profits from selling Lennox's house would go much further in Arizona than Atlanta. But that was a decision for another day, and wherever she landed, the fact remained that she needed to get serious about emptying the house.

As the coffee brewed and eggs fried in a pan, Dakota jumped an imaginary rope and boxed the air. By the time she finished breakfast, she was pumped and determined to have Lennox's house on the market before the end of the week.

She was stunned by how quickly the work went and chalked it up to the caffeine. Now that the hardest decision was made, the rest was easy. She spent the rest of the day working through the house one room at a time, ruthlessly dividing things into piles and packing the items she intended to keep into cardboard boxes. Not much ended up in those. She chose a few mementos from Kai's room, but it brought her a smile to bag up his toys, books, and clothing for the family shelter where other children could make good use of them.

By dinner, she had packed all the bedrooms but Lennox's office. She took a break for pizza, emptying kitchen drawers as she ate. The task soon spiraled out of hand. She had just cleaned out her fourth drawer when her phone rang.

Gina's upbeat voice greeted her. "Hey, Dakota. Do you mind if we get there a little early tomorrow? My first appointment just texted me to switch days, so I don't have anybody before you, and Allie is desperate to come over again."

Dakota laughed. "I don't know why. I'm not especially great with kids or anything."

"She's obsessed with your house. It sounds like she wants to play hide-and-seek with you? She's all excited about trying to find you."

"I don't mind at all. Should I pick anything up for her? Like... soda or candy?"

"Maybe some juice? She loves apple. I've been trying to keep her away from the soda monster."

"Noted. See you then."

Soda really was terrible, Dakota mused. Sugary. Addictive. Terrible for your teeth. Sweet. Caffeinated.

Exactly what she needed to power through the rest of the house.

She chugged a can from the fridge, then stalked up the stairs to tackle the place Lennox had spent the vast majority of his waking hours.

The work immediately slowed. His office wasn't filled with easily categorized personal effects. The desk was crammed full of receipts, tax documents, half-filled sketchbooks, and other disorganized papers. In the closet, she found a box of birthday cards going all the way back to the first year he'd become a Scott. It was no wonder his bedroom had taken her less than an hour to sort out. Everything that meant anything to Lennox at all was up here.

"Crap," she muttered, pushing away a narrow box that had originally held a computer monitor but was now inexplicably filled with Japanese candy and snack-size bags of chips. She stared around the room, searching for a foothold. If she could just find a place to start, she could get her inertia back.

She decided to work backward from newest to oldest. A stack of bills and unopened mail sat beside Lennox's keyboard. After selecting a bag of salt and vinegar chips from the goodie box, she settled into his chair and dove in.

Almost at the top, beneath his most recent power bill, Dakota found a sealed but unaddressed envelope. She assumed it was another one of his old birthday cards and nearly flicked it into the garbage like a playing card into a hat. She stopped just before it left her fingers.

Lennox's birthday had been months before. Whatever this was, he'd received it more recently than that.

Don't open it. You shouldn't read it.

Dakota hesitated. For some reason, this felt even more personal than sorting through his underclothes. Anything could be waiting in the envelope. Lennox could have had a romantic life he'd never told her about, and she could be about to view the last love letter he ever received. Gingerly, she opened the flap and pulled out a single folded sheet of notebook paper.

She was right. It was a letter.

And her name was scrawled across the top.

Chapter Eighteen

T he edge of the paper was rough and shredded where it had been ripped out of a spiral notebook. Her name was written in the top margin in blue ink, but the first few paragraphs had been written with a black ballpoint pen. After a gap, the blue reappeared.

Dakota's brow furrowed as she scanned the first section. At second glance, it didn't read like a letter. It was more like a stream-of-consciousness exercise, something he'd written in a journal and never intended anyone to see.

'I like the new curtains. Gina helped me put them up. Weird how much the darkness used to bother me. So much money wasted on new bulbs. The shadows are comforting. Don't know how I never noticed before. Maybe because of Kai? My sweet baby brother. He hated the dark. Screamed in it. Always scared of the Whisper Lady. Dakota was too. But she had a chance to grow out of it. Not like Kai. Fuck. Wish he had the chance. I hope he didn't die afraid. But I guess he would have been scared when he fell.

Can't stop thinking about her. The Whisper Lady. Maybe because it's dark? Or the shadows. There are so many now. Kai would hate it. Sometimes I think I hear him crying in his room but there's nothing in there when I check. God I miss that kid. Dakota too. Even when she's here it's not the same. I wish things could be how they were. But I don't even feel the same. Everything is different. It'll always be different.

They thought she was real. Maybe she was. And Kai really heard her. And Dakota really saw her. And she left before I could.'

Here, the ink changed to blue again, and Lennox's handwriting grew longer, each letter stretching wide before the next one began.

'Do you remember what you said when you heard her out your window? She wants me to find her. Can't stop thinking about that. Find her. If you went looking you would have died. Fallen just like Kai. But you came to me and we made her go away. I wonder why she came here. Kai saw her. She was here before he died. She was the reason. And she's the reason now. She won't let me out of the house. Never knew that before. Never knew it was her. Never knew that could happen.

I don't regret it though. I didn't know until now how I stopped her, but I'm glad I did. Even with how everything turned out for me. You got to grow up and that's what matters.'

The last two lines were nearly illegible. The letters wobbled as though they'd been drawn with a shaking hand, scribbled the way a child draws with a crayon.

'I can hear her now.

Don't listen.'

The letter was unsigned. Dakota read it again, skipping the black ink and focusing on the blue. Her heart ached for Lennox. She'd always known he struggled with his mental health. Her parents pushed him to talk to a therapist and see if he could improve his agoraphobia, but he never did. Even Dakota's prodding couldn't make him do it. He was happy with his life, or so they thought. The words he'd written painted a different picture, and she saw now that he was dwelling on Kai's death and her absence. In his grief over their departures, he turned to the same thing Dakota had. He started hearing voices in the dark.

The Whisper Lady.

If she let her thoughts blur, his logic almost came into focus like a Magic Eye poster. She could see the outline of them. Kai had started talking about the Whisper Lady, and then he died, and their family was thrown into chaos. The rest of them eventually recovered enough to function again. Enough, at least, to find their way back to some semblance of their lives and their routines.

Everyone except Lennox. He'd gone in the wrong direction.

From what Gina told her about when the curtains went up, he must have written this sometime in the last few weeks. Had he known how close he was to death? He had to have felt how ill he was. How weak.

In a way, she understood his unconscious reflex to blame his pain on the Whisper Lady. If he believed the same things Quinn did and thought there were supernatural beings out there who fed on negative emotions, it wouldn't have been a big leap to think someone like the Whisper Lady was causing all the unhappiness in his life.

Her abdomen sucked in, and before she could stop it, a sob snuck out. She wiped her face with both hands. She hated feeling like this, but it took genuine effort to rein herself in and stop crying. If she wasn't careful, she would end up like Lennox, so ruled by his emotions that he isolated himself in his house until his fear killed him.

With a final sniff, she stood and declared her chores done for the day. She trudged into her bedroom and climbed into bed, allowing only a few more tears to fall before drifting off into what she hoped would be better sleep than Quinn had gotten.

Chapter Nineteen

That night, Dakota's dreams felt like a memory. She had a few other memories like this, ones that had taken on a narrative in her mind. Unlike the brief flashes of moments that came to her as she had experienced them the first time around, these memories played out like a movie. In these, she saw herself from the outside.

As she slept, she watched her eight-year-old self huddle in her bed with her covers pulled up to her cheeks. Her wide, terrified eyes were locked on the window. Two silver circles blinked at her from the darkness.

Come find me. Kai wants me to show you something.

Once more, she saw her younger self go into Lennox's room. They snuck downstairs for the supplies he needed before sitting on his bedroom floor to make their Ouija board. After nothing moved the improvised planchette, Lennox smiled at her.

"See?" he said. "There's nothing out there. No ghosts. No monsters. Nothing to be afraid of. But you know what? Even if there was, I promise I'll protect you. I'll get right between you and anything that wants to hurt you and stop them from getting to you."

Young Dakota's narrow shoulders lifted as the weight of her anxiety evaporated. Lennox helped her to her feet, walked her to her room, and tucked her back into bed. Without the fear of the Whisper Lady holding her back, she promptly fell asleep.

What happened next wasn't a memory. At least, not one of her own.

As little Dakota slept, the tree outside her window cast shadows on the floor. Crooked lines swayed in the wind. Dakota inhaled. A shadow stretched toward her. It paused as she exhaled, creeping forward again as her chest filled.

One long finger, capped with a pointed nail, reached for Dakota's blanketed feet.

Then it howled.

The sound was a shrill cry that reverberated off the walls. Strangely, it woke no one in the Scott household, not even the child-Dakota who dozed in her bed. Only the Dakota who was watching through her dreams recognized the voice.

Still, she had never heard the Whisper Lady scream.

Some unseen force jerked the Whisper Lady away from the bed and thrust her through the wall between Dakota's and Lennox's rooms. Adult Dakota's disembodied form followed, pausing in Lennox's closet to watch through the crack in the door, terrified of seeing the Whisper Lady as anything more solid than shadow.

Though her screeching continued, the Whisper Lady remained a dark haze. Her pointed nails gouged scratches in Lennox's rug as she was dragged across the floor toward his bed. Each time he inhaled, she lost more ground.

When she reached his mouth, Lennox gasped. His muscles shuddered and spasmed. His back arched off the mattress. The last bit of the Whisper Lady's wail cut off as she disappeared down his gullet.

All was still. The bulb in his bedside light flickered to life and cast a comforting glow across the room. Adult Dakota emerged from the closet and tiptoed toward the bed.

Lennox opened his eyes. At first, he didn't speak. He didn't even breathe. His body didn't move, but his head jerked toward her, millimeter by millimeter like the second hand of a ticking clock until he was looking straight at her.

His lips parted. "I couldn't remember what happened until I started hearing her again. I kept her inside as long as I could, Dakota. But I can't protect you anymore." He smiled sadly. "I can't protect anyone."

Chapter Twenty

Dakota woke with a gasp. Sweat soaked the sheet beneath her, but she didn't feel overheated. She was chilled to the core.

Her feet slipped on the hardwood floor as she scrambled out of bed and rushed down the hallway to Lennox's office. She dropped to her knees on the rug and pushed aside the boxes and piles she'd been sorting through earlier. Once the rug was clean, she traced her fingertips over the rough fabric.

There. Six lines, deep but fine, drew a path that would have pointed from the closet to Lennox's bed. They were separated into two pairs of three, with a three-foot gap between each set. Dakota fit her hands over them and shivered. The spacing left no doubt.

That was no dream. All of it had happened, exactly the way she had seen it.

Lennox had done as he'd promised. He had protected her from the Whisper Lady by using his own body as a mousetrap. The trap had ensnared her when she went for

Dakota. That was the reason he'd been afraid of the dark, even as an adult. The Whisper Lady was an ever-present fixture in his life, terrifying him from the inside out.

That fear had only gone away a few weeks ago. From his letter, that was when he started to hear the Whisper Lady. Why? Was it because he was growing weaker?

Was she *making* him grow weaker?

Horror flooded upward from Dakota's toes and into her mouth. She fell onto all fours, and her twisting stomach heaved. Yes, that was exactly what the Whisper Lady had done. Ever since Lennox had trapped her, she had been pounding on her prison from within, scratching and clawing until the walls crumbled enough for her to escape.

And Lennox hadn't known what was happening until it was too late.

Dakota's head spun. Too much of her reality was being pulverized at once. She couldn't keep up. As she struggled to sort through it all, a single truth kept snapping to the top of the pile.

The Whisper Lady was real.

And if Lennox hadn't unwittingly trapped her twenty years before, Dakota would have been her next victim. The Whisper Lady would have killed her, just like Kai. Some night, Dakota would've listened to the voice that told her to climb out the window. She would have gone outside in search of the demon that crooked its shadowy finger at her in the night. But what did she want?

Her brain struggled past the shroud of whiskey that veiled unremembered pieces of her dinner with Gina and Quinn. Quinn's reaction to the homemade Ouija board had hammered home his belief in the supernatural, but the full details of his theories didn't surface until her forehead rested on the Whisper Lady's claw marks. He had talked about the things demons want, their inhuman appetites, their desire to gorge themselves on negative emotions.

"The stronger, the better," he'd said.

Like anyone, Dakota had felt hundreds of emotions at nearly every intensity. Joy, rejection, euphoria, disappointment, contentment. But in the grand scheme of her life, there were three that penetrated the deepest and stuck with her the longest. They were the ones that permeated her dreams and woke her in the middle of the night. The ones that colored every day, every memory, every moment.

Grief. Guilt. Shame.

From the minute her father told her Lennox had passed, those emotions had weighed on her. They'd gotten worse since she had come back to this house. Every second she spent here, the burden grew heavier. She could feel it pressing down around her from all sides. Whether she was thinking about Lennox or not thinking about him, whether she was considering moving back to Astoria or planning to sell the house, whether she was packing up his things or wallowing on the couch, those feelings were there, poking at her from the shadows.

Or rather, *she* was there.

Dakota could hear her voice now. It slithered through the cracks in the floorboards and coiled around her, whispering strange comforts one moment and demeaning her the next. She knew it was the same voice that had lured Kai down the back stairwell. It was the same voice Lennox had talked about in his letter. The same one that had called to Dakota from outside her bedroom window. They had all heard it.

But had their parents?

Even now, twenty years after the fact, Dakota's heart broke to think of Kai. But what she felt was nothing compared to the grief and sorrow that had broken Kerry and Gaelle Scott.

Yes, she decided. Her parents had heard the Whisper Lady. Not the sweet voice of sympathy that tried to convince Dakota to stay here until she rotted away like Lennox. Not the childlike invitation to come out and play. Just an incessant jackhammer of remorse that only stopped when Lennox trapped the Whisper Lady inside of himself.

She wasn't trapped anymore. She was out, sneaking through the shadows, slipping her poisonous tongue into Dakota's mind.

And, Dakota realized with horror, Allie's.

"*Allie's been hassling me all day,*" Gina had said at the restaurant. "*She keeps telling me, 'I want to play in the basement with that lady.'*"

The Whisper Lady hadn't been trying to get Dakota's attention the day Allie had gone into the basement. The beckoning finger was meant for one person and one person alone. Just as the Whisper Lady had first reached out to Kai, she was once again targeting the youngest person within her reach.

And Allie had already heard the deadly invitation.

Dakota struggled to her feet. Her frantic hands rummaged through letters and boxes, hunting for her cell phone. She'd left it somewhere in here, and she had never needed it so badly in her life.

Stop worrying, came a whisper. *Your imagination is running away with you again. Allie will be fine.*

"No!" Dakota shouted at the walls.

She knew now who that voice belonged to. It didn't come from within her own mind. It came from the shadows where the Whisper Lady lived. The demon was good at impersonating Dakota's internal monologue, but her tricks wouldn't work anymore.

With a shout of victory, Dakota yanked her phone out from the gap between Lennox's seat cushion and the armrest. The display read a few minutes after eleven o'clock. She hadn't been asleep for long, but it was already late enough that a child Allie's age would be in bed.

She's safe there. If there's danger, it's only here in this
house. Nothing can harm her at home.

Even if she hadn't known where that silky voice was
really coming from, Dakota would have recognized the
lie. The Whisper Lady escaped the moment Lennox died.
Within hours, she had found Dakota in Atlanta. She had
watched Dakota from the dark corners of the bathroom.

The light had burned out that morning, Dakota remembered. More and more burned out each day here. If
the demon could do that, if she could travel across the
country, what was the Whisper Lady capable of doing to a
little girl just a few blocks away?

Dakota had no idea, and that scared her more than anything.

With no real plan in mind except telling Allie not to listen to the whispers, she dialed Gina. Her fingers drummed
impatiently on Lennox's desk as the phone rang.

"Hi, you've reached Regina Queen of Clean. To sched-
ule—"

"Shit." Dakota hung up and pounded the top of her cell
phone against her forehead. "Shit, shit, shit."

Panic gripped her mind and her body, but instead of
holding her still, it shook her like soda in a bottle. She
might explode any second. Her knees bounced, and her
mind churned. Inaction was not an option. She couldn't
rely on the phone. If she wanted to know Allie was safe,
if she wanted any hope of explaining such inexplicable

dangers to Gina, she had to go there in person. And she had to go right now.

Lennox's death and the responsibility of handling his affairs would have overwhelmed and immobilized her even without the Whisper Lady's influence. But neither the couch nor her bed called to her anymore. She raced down the stairs, snatched her car key off the hook, and bolted out the door.

It slammed shut behind her, and as she clicked the button on the fob to unlock her car, her eyes widened. Her head jerked back toward the house.

She had only grabbed her car key. Lennox's key still hung on the hook inside the door.

Out of reflex, she spun around and tried the handle. It didn't move. She had locked the door behind herself.

An expletive she rarely used settled on the tip of her tongue, but she swallowed it back. Getting locked out of her house wouldn't stop her from saving Allie. She could easily smash a rock through the kitchen window when she got back from doing what she needed to do.

As she backed out of the driveway and sped down the street, she dialed Gina again. This time, she waited for the outgoing voicemail message to finish. "Gina, it's Dakota. Call me back. It's an emergency. Allie could be in danger, and—"

A tone beeped in her ear. Gina was already calling back on the other line.

"Hey Dakota. Is everything okay?" Gina's voice lowered. "Quinn's over, so—"

"You have to go check on Allie," Dakota interrupted. She slowed at a stop sign just long enough to glance in both directions before blowing past it. "Something's after her."

"What are you talking about? Allie's asleep."

"That doesn't mean she's safe!" Dakota wrenched the car around a corner. "Just humor me, okay? Check on her. And turn on all the lights in the house."

Quinn's low voice carried through from the background. "What's wrong?"

"Dakota says something's after Allie."

There was a brief scuffling on the other end of the line before Quinn spoke again, louder this time. "Is it the thing I felt in your house?"

"Yes. And she wants Allie."

"We're headed to her room right now."

If Dakota's adrenaline wasn't so high, Quinn's immediate understanding of the situation would have come as a relief. But she couldn't relax yet. Not until she knew the Whisper Lady hadn't somehow lured Allie out onto a window ledge like she'd tried to do to Dakota twenty years before.

She needed to know. "Is her room on the second floor?"

"No." Quinn didn't question her reason for asking. "It's a basement apartment."

That made Dakota feel an ounce better. She couldn't see how Allie could get hurt in a basement. But she still pressed down on the accelerator, driving to the sounds of hurried footsteps and the creaking hinges of a door.

"Allie?" Gina's voice was panicked. "Where are you?"

"The window is open," Quinn said. "Did she go outside?"

Dakota's heart sank. The car slowed. She was too late. The Whisper Lady had gotten to Allie. Somehow, she had found a way. Now she was going to crack Gina open like a coconut and feast on her sorrow.

Gina would find Allie any moment. Dakota couldn't take bearing witness to that, couldn't handle hearing Gina scream the way Dakota's mother must have screamed when she found Kai. Her phone slipped down her palm, and her thumb searched for the button to hang up the call.

"Wait. She left a note." Quinn's voice stilled Dakota's hand. "It says, 'She told me to come play.'"

"Fuck!" Dakota slammed on her brakes and cranked the wheel for a U-turn.

The Whisper Lady was a crafty bitch. She would give her that. Why destroy one woman with grief when you could have two? Allie wasn't Dakota's daughter, but it would break Dakota all the same if something happened to that girl.

Especially if it happened in the same place they'd lost Kai.

Chapter Twenty-One

The rental car's tires screeched as Dakota jerked to a stop in the driveway. More curses flowed from her mouth as she fumbled with her seatbelt, finally freeing herself and scrambling up the walk. Her instincts drew her toward the back stairwell. That was where the Whisper Lady first struck, and with the front door locked, it was her best chance at taking Allie.

She stopped as her mind registered that something was off.

The front door hung open.

Dakota was sure she had locked it. She remembered trying to get back in. But just as the Whisper Lady had unlocked the back gate for Kai, she had opened the door for Allie.

"Allie!" she shouted, bursting into the house. "Allie!"

Nothing.

Dakota frantically scanned the space for any sign of the girl. Her gaze landed on the basement door. The thinnest crack of black was visible at the edge.

"I want to play in the basement with that lady."

She ripped the door open. The light switch didn't respond. She tapped on her phone's flashlight and swept it down the stairs.

Allie lay facedown at the bottom, thin limbs twisted at unnatural angles.

Chapter Twenty-Two

D akota's heels slipped as she stumbled down the stairs. She lost her balance, and her knees cracked against the hard concrete floor. She didn't register the pain. Her fingers were on Allie's neck, every nerve and sense hunting for any sign of life. She didn't have much hope, but—

Allie rasped a shallow breath.

An enormous sigh left Dakota's lungs, and she refilled them with a deep inhale of the damp, dusty basement air.

"It's okay," she murmured to Allie as she dialed 9-1-1. "You're going to be okay."

The ambulance arrived a few minutes before Gina and Quinn did. Dakota decided that was a small mercy, a tiny morsel of anguish ripped out from under from the Whisper Lady's clutches. By the time Gina saw her daughter, Allie was already strapped to a stretcher, oxygen mask over her small face, gravely injured but still alive.

"I'm riding with her," Gina told the paramedics. It wasn't a question but a demand, and they made no argument.

Quinn sprinted down the driveway after her to snatch her keys from her hand. "I'll follow you guys."

He and Dakota watched the ambulance pull away from the curb. It headed for Columbia Memorial, sirens blazing. Dakota's body shook. The air was wet and cold, but she knew that had nothing to do with the goosebumps and trembling muscles running from her head to her toes.

"Are you alright?" Quinn asked.

"Fine," she answered automatically. She caught sight of his dubious eyebrow, and her vision clouded with tears. "Not fine. This is all my fault."

"You know that's not true. We both know what really did this." He pursed his lips. After a moment, he said, "But Gina doesn't. By the time I calmed her down enough to get her into the car, she was asking how you could do this to her."

Shame and guilt shivered down Dakota's spine. She hadn't been the one to trip Allie on the stairs, but she may as well have been. It had taken her too long to see the truth. She hadn't been able to save Allie. And whether or not Allie survived the night, the Whisper Lady got what she wanted.

Dakota stared into the shadows left behind by the ambulance's departure. A pair of shining silver eyes stared back. The bottoms of the circles curved inward, pushed up by the smiling cheeks of a demon in the midst of a good meal.

"You should go," she told Quinn. "Gina needs you."

He nodded and started for the street, then paused and turned back. "I don't think it's safe for you to be here. Especially not alone. Here." He dropped a hotel keycard into her hand. "I'll stay at the hospital with Allie and Gina. You can have my room tonight."

She gripped the keycard in her hand. Its fine edges dug into her skin. "Sure. Thanks."

Quinn left, and Dakota turned back to the shadows. No eyes lingered there. She was sure the Whisper Lady had gone back inside, down into the basement to digest the fear, pain, and horror she had inflicted on everyone who had stepped foot in the house tonight.

Dakota pocketed the keycard and trudged up the walk to the house. It didn't matter where she went. The Whisper Lady would follow her, just as she had followed Allie to her house and found Dakota in Atlanta. Here in Astoria, the demon had stalked Dakota's steps to the mortuary and the cemetery.

Wherever Dakota went, the Whisper Lady would be there. Dakota grimly ran the odds on whether the demon's next target would be someone in her life or Dakota herself. Haunting Dakota would certainly give the demon a reliable meal ticket time and again, taking away the people she cared about one by one.

The thought drew Dakota to a halt on the porch.

If a leech found somewhere to feed, it didn't eat a little then dash away to sample another creature. It stayed there, only detaching when it was fully sated.

There was a reason the Whisper Lady hadn't left the Scott house after killing Kai. Their family was too delicious a feast. Gaelle and Kerry's grief over losing a child was stronger than anything Dakota had ever felt. It would be impossible for the demon to resist, and the Whisper Lady was ruled by gluttony. She would target the Scotts again and again, stabbing at them from the darkness to intensify their sorrow as she constructed her traps for claiming the rest of their children.

Dakota shuddered. If Lennox hadn't imprisoned the demon inside of himself, Dakota would be dead. And once she was gone, the Whisper Lady would have come for Lennox. She had gotten what she wanted, just slightly out of order. Dakota wondered how difficult the decision had been—stay here with Dakota, or follow the Scotts back to Arizona, where she could continue to feed on the loss of their son.

After a moment, Dakota saw that it would have been easy to decide. If the Whisper Lady could keep Dakota here in the house, convince her to stay in Astoria, then drain her until she died the same way Lennox had, the

Scotts would have no choice but to come back here once more. Their grief over losing their third and final child in the same house where they'd lost the first two, the same house where they'd raised a family and hoped to raise more.... It would be too much for anyone to handle. It would pierce the souls of Dakota's parents far more deeply than if Dakota died anywhere else.

Since waking from her dream, Dakota had thought Lennox was the trap. Whether or not he had intended to, she assumed Lennox had woven his net with the Ouija board, letter by letter, promise by promise. But the Whisper Lady schemed further ahead than any human was capable of doing, and Lennox's actions had been nothing but a temporary roadblock.

The demon was the true architect of the mousetrap. Little by little, she had constructed it in and around the Scott family. Lennox's death was the cheese, placed delicately on the catch to lure her family back to the place where their grief echoed the strongest. Allie had stumbled into it completely by accident, but the Whisper Lady wasn't about to pass up a good meal.

Dakota reached for the door handle. She could only see one path forward. The Whisper Lady may have built the trap, but it wasn't too late to turn things around. There was a way to stop her from doing any more damage to Dakota's family.

At least for a little while.

Chapter Twenty-Three

A spray of blood tattooed the concrete floor where Allie had cracked her head. Dakota stepped around it, Mouse Trap and flashlight in hand.

She wasn't exactly sure what she was doing. But she had an outcome in mind, and she remembered everything Lennox had said and done the last time the game had been used. She suspected Quinn's warning against using the Ouija board alone was to prevent a spirit from getting out of control. Dakota didn't need to worry about that. She wasn't trying to have a conversation with the demon.

The Whisper Lady's conversations tended to be one-sided, anyway.

Dakota settled onto the floor. Condensation from the furnace dripped into the drain from the pipe beside her with a soft *plip-plip-plip*. She set the flashlight on its end, pointed at the ceiling, and opened the game. Lennox's Ouija board waited on the inside of the cover, and the blue

plastic cage peeked out from the jumble of trap compo-
nents and game pieces. She pushed the rest of the game
aside and placed the cage facedown on the letter W.

"For Whisper Lady," she murmured.

She placed the pointer and index fingers from each of
her hands on the edges of the trap. Her body tensed. She
was suddenly terrified of the crude planchette jerking and
spasming across the board on its own.

When nothing moved, she let out a breath.

"I am speaking to the entity that lives in this house,"
she said, voice echoing off the unfinished walls. "I don't
know your name. My brothers called you the Whisper
Lady. Whoever or whatever you are, I know you're out
there."

A sound like fabric swishing across a concrete floor rose
up from the edges of the room. Dakota felt it more than
heard it, sensed the icy breeze swirling around her in every
direction. She shivered.

The planchette fluttered beneath her fingertips.

*You're nothing more than a frightened child. You won't
find me down here. I'm not of this world. You must find me
in the stars. Look for me from the rooftops.*

Dakota tensed. The argument was just logical enough
that one foot twitched toward the stairs. She grounded it
beneath her thighs. That trick was twenty years old. She
had resisted it then. She could resist it now.

Is this how you pictured your life? So unsatisfying that you would consider abandoning it and moving across the country? It must be exhausting.

The words stung. Much as Dakota hated to admit it, the demon was right about that.

Your father left many things down here when he gave up on your family. Drink one to find me. I can show you a never-ending happiness.

Dakota hated herself for considering it, even for the millisecond that the thought of drinking paint thinner lingered in her mind. She exhaled slowly and let it go.

Something fluttered at the back of her head. The whispers grew stronger, but the words were indistinct. Dakota winced. Pain and pressure crowded her skull. She had the sudden sensation of fingertips pressing along her thoughts, tapping and testing for weak spots.

The Whisper Lady was invading her mind.

Rather than fear, triumph flooded Dakota's body. There was a connection between them now. The moment Dakota perceived it, she seized on it and drew the Whisper Lady closer.

"I've already found you. Show yourself."

The demon struggled against her. She felt it pulling back, trying to wrench its tendrils away. Dakota yanked harder. She refused to lose this tug-of-war.

Out from the shadows, the Whisper Lady crept. Her round eyes reflected the light, and she blinked against it, recoiling from the brightness. After a moment, she slithered forward again, hunched so much that her forelimbs dragged along the floor. Three long fingers curled outward from each hand. They were thin, bending at three too many joints and ending in pointed nails that scraped the concrete with a low *hisssssss*. Shadows clouded the rest of her body. She was intertwined with the darkness. Part of it. Inseparable from it.

Dakota's joints locked in place. Her thoughts skipped and repeated. This was something no human had been meant to see, something that was supposed to live at the barest edges of her vision. Her mind abandoned any expectation of processing it. She forced her eyes closed.

It was easier to focus now. With a firm grasp on the Whisper Lady, Dakota pictured Lennox as he had been the night he trapped her. All Dakota had to do now was follow in his footsteps. She needed to pledge herself to stopping the demon from preying on anyone else.

"I promise I'll protect...." Dakota faltered. "I will protect...."

Who was left for her to shield? The demon had taken Kai. It had taken Lennox. It had devastated her family and had destroyed her friendship with Gina. She'd been too late to protect Allie. It remained to be seen if the girl would survive the night. Everything and everyone around her had already been shattered by the Whisper Lady's machinations.

There was nothing whole that Dakota could protect now. But she would still defend what fragments remained as much as she could.

Still, it was one thing to say she would lay down her life for someone. It was another thing entirely to stare down the demon after seeing what it had done to Lennox. If Dakota succeeded, she would turn inward, slowly imploding until there was nothing left to hold up her weary bones.

All she was doing was buying time.

"*I don't regret it,*" Lennox had said in his letter.

If he didn't look back, neither would she.

She leaned her head back, inhaled, and opened herself up to the demon. As she felt it flowing toward her, inch by inch, breath by breath, a sudden sense of freedom washed over her. All her life, she had been tamping down her emotions. Stuffing them into boxes. Burying them deep inside. She was always worried about how they would make her look to other people. And after that terrible year where the Whisper Lady held sway over the entire Scott household, Dakota had instinctively shied away from letting her feelings bring anyone down.

There was no point in holding anything back now. Once the demon was inside her, she would never feel like herself again. In the few breaths she had left before her life, her mind, and her body changed forever, she wanted to savor the things that were truly hers.

Tears shimmered on her eyelids before raining down her cheeks. Her body shook. Her breath came in ragged sobs. She cradled her torso with her arms. Why hadn't she hugged Kai more while he was alive? What would he have been like if he'd had a chance to grow up? She wished she'd had more time with him. She would give anything to see him again.

And Lennox. How many times had she noticed how much weight he'd lost when she visited? What was the moment she gave up on trying to help him break free of the chains that kept him tethered to this house? If she had worked harder, if she had tried longer, she could have held onto him.

The demon was close now. Its teeth grated along Dakota's skin, and its tongue lapped up what sorrow it could before Dakota locked her away.

Dakota didn't feel any of it. She grieved for Allie, the bright little girl who loved everything eerie and who might never see another day. She mourned the friendship she could have had with Gina and the loss of her relationships in Georgia. Once the demon took hold, she would become like Lennox, and everyone outside these walls would fall away.

Last of all, she wept for her parents. If they outlived her, their grief would drown their entire world. When they came to see her, they would sense how withdrawn she had become. They would know she was following Lennox down his doleful path, but they wouldn't know why, and they wouldn't be able to stop it. A wail rose up in her chest. They didn't deserve any of this. She wanted more for them than their life had become.

A sudden light flickered through Dakota's eyelids. She fluttered them open and wiped her sleeve across her face, leaving a smear of tears and mucus on her cheeks.

The room was bright. She blinked against the bare bulb above her, which blazed more brilliantly than it ever had before. Her tears dried. For the first time since she had found Allie, she saw the room clearly.

Few shadows remained. Around her, the demon's wispy form sputtered and writhed on the floor. One three-fingered claw wrapped around Dakota's waist. Its grip weakened with every tear that dripped from Dakota's chin, but as Dakota craned her neck, she saw that the demon's mouth was clamped on the side of her throat, wet teeth dripping saliva down her shoulder.

At once, Dakota saw the flaw in her mental image of the Whisper Lady. She wasn't a leech. She wouldn't ever be satisfied enough to fall off on her own. No, the demon would keep feeding, gorging until she burst.

Dakota let go of the last few emotional restraints she had left. Everything she had ever held back poured out of her. They surged like floodwater from a broken levee. Regret over every mistake. Chagrin from every awkward interaction or flubbed game. Anger and frustration at work. Loneliness at home. Rage. Sadness. Disgust. Sorrow. Shame.

The Whisper Lady swallowed it all. She wouldn't stop. She didn't know how. And if she took in any more, she would burst like an overfilled tick.

Dakota's brightness grew. It chased the shadows from even the deepest corners. Still, it wasn't enough. The demon kept drinking, its last, faint tendril clinging to the most exquisite meal it had ever tasted.

The bulb above them flickered.

A final sob shook Dakota's body. The bulb was on the edge of burning out. When it did, she wouldn't be able to hold the Whisper Lady back. She would be swallowed by shadows. There would be no coming back.

The light dimmed.

She had failed. The demon had won.

Then, Dakota's grief for herself, for the choice she had been forced to make and for the life she would never have, flared into a supernova.

The demon swelled, then burst. Dakota's light blasted every speck of shadows into nothingness.

Along with the darkness, the Whisper Lady vanished.

Chapter
Twenty-Four

Dakota supervised as the movers carried her furniture into her new home. She inspected the headboard and the dresser once they'd been deposited in the master bedroom, checking for any signs of damage from the long, cross-country journey.

It had taken her a few weeks to finally make a decision about Lennox's house. In the end, she had packed up her life in Georgia and headed west.

She pulled out a stick of lip balm and smeared it on her lips. The dry desert air was already wreaking havoc on her skin. Her parents assured her she would adjust to the Arizona climate, but the basket full of moisturizer and body butter they'd given her made her doubt their words.

The smell of her peach lotion mingled with the scent of grilled chicken from the yard next door. Dakota's empty stomach growled, and her mind turned to the welcome dinner her parents were making. Their sprawling ranch house was just a few minutes away, close enough for frequent visits.

Quinn had tried to convince her to make a life in Astoria, to sell Lennox's house and buy something of her own. He argued that Allie would benefit from talking through her trauma with someone who had faced the Whisper Lady head on. But Dakota agreed with Gina that it was better for Allie if she was never reminded of what really happened that night. As she healed, the girl could explain away the reasons she had ventured into the basement in whatever way her mind saw fit.

Even if Gina hadn't asked her to leave, Dakota wouldn't have stayed. It was too close to where the demon had first gouged devastating wounds into the Scott family's souls. Dakota wanted to be here, in the place her parents had found a new happiness, enjoying their company in what precious time they all had left.

She savored the knowledge that from now on, her feelings would only be feelings. Her emotions would be her own, not created or amplified by any dark forces. She would feel them, process them, and experience them evolving as time went by.

Never again would they be devoured.

The movers left. Dakota surveyed the taped-up boxes and shuffled a few between rooms. It felt right to put Lennox and Kai's mementos in the guest bedroom. She imagined them coming to visit and saw their delighted smiles when they found the things they loved on display. Sorrow twisted in her stomach, but it was lighter now. Less debilitating. And at the edges, the first rays of fond memories rose like the sun to overtake the darkness.

Acknowledgements

I don't know why these are always so hard. Maybe it's because I have so many wonderful and supportive people in my life, and I'm worried I'll leave someone out. So let me begin by saying this list is far from complete.

First, I wrote *Mouse Trap* immediately after yet another seizure. Epilepsy is a jerk, guys. I would say that "somehow" I was able to be productive in the weeks that followed, but it's no mystery how I did it. Thank you, Kelly, for getting me through that time the way you get me through everything, and for listening to me mutter to myself about these characters before letting me read you the entire book, pausing after every chapter to demand feedback. You're amazing. I love you.

Thank you, Mom and Dad, for critiquing my query letter and reassuring me that the premise sounded awesome. You've always been my biggest fans, and you guys get all the credit for exposing me to so many horror books and movies that I started creating my own.

This book literally wouldn't exist without C.R. Langille and Timber Ghost Press. When I was first bouncing ideas for a quiet horror novella off C.R. at a conference, I didn't dare dream that they would want to publish it. Thanks so much for taking a chance on me!

Thank you, Beverley, for your fabulous edits. I feel so lucky that even though I'm working with a new-to-me publisher, I somehow still got to work with you!

And as always, thank you—yes, *you*—for reading this book. I'm genuinely honored you chose to spend your time in my head like this. Thank you, thank you, thank you.

About the Author

Caryn Larrinaga is an internationally best-selling mystery and horror author. She has won multiple awards for her work, including the League of Utah Writers Gold Typewriter and the Cat Writers Association Muse Medallion. In 2021, she was named Writer of the Year by the League of Utah Writers.

In addition to her novels and short story collections, Caryn has written for tabletop RPGs, podcasts, literary journals, newspapers, and zines. Her work has been adapted for audio, short films, and a forthcoming animation. Her spooky supernatural whodunit, DONN'S HILL, topped the Amazon best seller lists for psychic mysteries and cozy animal mysteries.

Watching scary movies through split fingers terrified Caryn as a child, and those nightmares inspire her to write now. Her 90-year-old house has a colorful history, and the creaking walls and narrow hallways send her running (never walking) up the stairs. Exploring her fears through writing makes Caryn feel a little less foolish for wanting a buddy to accompany her into the tool shed.

Caryn lives near Salt Lake City, Utah, with her husband and their clowder of cats. She is an active member of Science Fiction and Fantasy Writers of America, the Horror Writers Association, the Cat Writers Association, and the League of Utah Writers. Visit www.carynlarrinaga.com for free short fiction and true tales of haunted places.

If you enjoyed, *Mouse Trap*, please consider leaving a review on Amazon or Goodreads. Reviews help the author and the press.

If you go to www.timberghostpress.com you can sign up for our newsletter so you can stay up-to-date on all our upcoming titles, plus you'll get informed of new horror flash fiction and poetry featured on our site monthly.

Take care and thanks for reading, *Mouse Trap* by Caryn Larrinaga.

-Timber Ghost Press

Printed in Great Britain
by Amazon